SIMON & SCHUSTER CHILDREN'S PUBLISHING

ADVANCE READER'S COPY

TITLE: Gigi Shin Is Not a Nerd

AUTHOR: Lyla Lee

IMPRINT: Aladdin

ON-SALE DATE: 03/05/2024

ISBN: 9781665939171

FORMAT: Middle-Grade Fiction Hardcover

PRICE: US $17.99 / $22.99 CAN

AGES: 8 to 12

PAGES: 176

Please send any review or mention of this book to
ChildrensPublicity@simonandschuster.com.

Aladdin • Atheneum Books for Young Readers
Beach Lane Books • Beyond Words • Boynton Bookworks
Caitlyn Dlouhy Books • Denene Millner Books
Libros para niños • Little Simon • Margaret K. McElderry Books
MTV Books • Paula Wiseman Books • Salaam Reads
Simon & Schuster Books for Young Readers
Simon Pulse • Simon Spotlight

ALSO BY LYLA LEE

FOR YOUNGER READERS
The Mindy Kim series

FOR YA READERS
I'll Be the One
Flip the Script

Gigi Shin Is Not a Nerd

LYLA LEE

ALADDIN

New York   London   Toronto   Sydney   New Delhi

ALADDIN

An imprint of Simon & Schuster Children's Publishing Division

1230 Avenue of the Americas, New York, New York 10020

First Aladdin hardcover edition March 2024

Text copyright © 2024 by Lyla Lee

Jacket illustrations copyright © 2024 by Karyn Lee

All rights reserved, including the right of reproduction in whole or in part in any form.

ALADDIN and related logo are registered trademarks of Simon & Schuster, Inc.

Simon & Schuster: Celebrating 100 Years of Publishing in 2024

For information about special discounts for bulk purchases, please contact Simon & Schuster Special Sales at 1-866-506-1949 or business@simonandschuster.com.

The Simon & Schuster Speakers Bureau can bring authors to your live event. For more information or to book an event contact the Simon & Schuster Speakers Bureau at 1-866-248-3049 or visit our website at www.simonspeakers.com.

Jacket designed by Laura DiSiena and Irene Vandervoort

Interior designed by Irene Vandervoort

The text of this book was set in Tellumo.

Manufactured in the United States of America 0124 BVG

2 4 6 8 10 9 7 5 3 1

Library of Congress Cataloging-in-Publication Data TK

ISBN 9781665939171 (hc)

ISBN 9781665939195 (ebook)

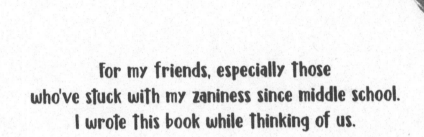

For my friends, especially those
who've stuck with my zaniness since middle school.
I wrote this book while thinking of us.

One

Seventh-grade choir is a time to sing for most people, but not for me. I sit in the very back, with my music binder up in front of my face. And when it's not time for me to sing, I draw.

When I put pencil to paper, everything around me fades away except the lines and curves I mark on the page. Even the loud banging of Mr. Martin's piano became muffled as I worked on my latest comic book panel about Meteor Girl, one of my newest characters.

When you live in a quiet and boring suburban town like me, and your family isn't rich enough to go to cool places like Europe or Colorado like your friends do during breaks, there isn't much else to do to entertain yourself. Drawing is how I have adventures without having to pay a single cent. I may not be able to fly super fast across the night sky as Gigi Shin, but as Meteor Girl, I could fly over the Pyramids of Giza and the Eiffel Tower.

"Gigi?" said Mr. Martin, the choir director. "What did I say about drawing in choir?"

I looked up only to find myself staring right into the teacher's eyes. Thankfully, he was still behind the piano with both hands on the keyboard—sometimes, when he feels "inspired," he walks up and down the rows—but he looked so mad that I could picture laser beams shooting out of his eyes.

That's when I realized that everyone else in the class was standing up except me. No wonder Mr. Martin could tell I was drawing again.

Oops! I quickly stood and held my choir binder higher up so it was covering my face. A few people behind me snickered, but I didn't look. I was scared of Mr. Martin but not of the other kids in my grade. They already laughed at me plenty last year, when I tried giving myself a chic bob like the ladies in the fashion magazines but gave myself an asymmetrical, crooked haircut that only went to my ears instead. Compared to that, this was nothing.

My hair hadn't fully recovered from that disaster, so I was

still wearing a headband now. But it was okay. Headbands were coming back into style. And my red headband with white polka dots was especially cute. It went well with my white silk scarf and red overalls. I managed to get all sorts of cool clothes from the thrift stores in our neighborhood. I loved making my own style!

"Sorry, Mr. Martin," I said. "I'll make sure to pay extra attention for the rest of class."

I snuck a glance at the binder of the girl next to me and saw that we were singing "Do-Re-Mi" from *The Sound of Music*. I flipped to the song. It was easy enough to find since Mr. Martin always printed our sheet music in different colors so we could instantly tell which song was in which packet.

Mr. Martin sighed and shook his head before finally looking away from me. "Okay, class, let's start again from the top. *Doe, a deer* . . ."

Like I promised Mr. Martin, I put all my effort into singing, and class went by fast after that. Choir is sort of pointless when you are tone-deaf like me, but it was the only class I could take to fill our school's music requirement. After all, it wasn't like I could draw while holding a violin or a trumpet. So, even though I hate it, I try to do my best in choir when I'm not drawing.

While I was singing—or trying to sing—I happened to

accidentally make eye contact with Paul Kim Wiley, one of the most popular boys in our grade. It was hard not to since the choir chairs formed a U, and as a bass, he was on the exact opposite side of me. When our eyes met, he smiled, and I hid my face with my binder so he couldn't see me blush.

Paul was half white, but he had a Korean mom like me. We were friends when we were kids since we used to go to the same Korean school, but he stopped going when we started middle school. So we barely talked anymore. He was kinda annoying when we were little, but as a seventh grader, he was cute and nice. All the girls in choir whispered about how he was like a kid K-pop star: great at singing and super polite. He was also on the seventh-grade football team, which made him the closest possible thing to a prince in a Texan school like ours.

When the bell rang, I gathered my things. Next period was art, my all-time favorite. I was so excited that I rushed to the door, not looking where I was going until it was too late.

"Oof!"

I glanced up to see that I'd run smack-dab into Paul. Paul was now a head taller than me, so he had to look down to meet my gaze.

"Oh, sorry, Gigi," he said, even though *I'd* run into *him*.

"It's okay," my mouth replied. I was so nervous that my

brain was taking a while to catch up. It was weird how back in Korean school, Paul and I used to mess around and chat effortlessly every week. Now things were so awkward between us, I could barely say two—or three, depending on how you count it—words to him!

"Where are you headed off to?" Paul asked, and it took me a couple of seconds to process what he'd asked.

"Oh, art," I said, almost robotically. "It's my favorite class."

"Oh yeah, I always see you drawing during choir," Paul replied with a smile. "You're really good! I've seen your art on display in the hallway by the art class all the time."

My jaw almost dropped to the floor. "You've looked at my art?"

A funny look crossed over Paul's face, and his cheeks reddened just a bit. "Yeah, one of my friends is also in art, so we meet up together in that area sometimes."

I *had* seen Paul meet up with Caleb, a boy in my class, a couple of times. But I had no idea Paul had even been remotely interested in our artwork.

"Cool," I replied, because that was the only thing I could think of saying. "Well, see you around!"

"See you!" Paul turned and walked away, sounding like he was as glad as I was that our awkward conversation was over.

If I had any other class next, I would have been too

mortified by what had just happened between Paul and me to focus. But sixth period was art, so I pretty much forgot about everything else by the time I stepped into the hallway. Art was the class I share with my best friends, Zeina Hassan and Carolina Garcia. This was the first time the three of us had a class together since fourth grade, so it was awesome.

On my way to the art room, I met up with Zeina, who was coming from English class. Zeina is the first friend I made when I moved to Bluebonnet in kindergarten. We're next-door neighbors, so we grew up making mud pies when we were little and riding our bikes to the library to read manga in fifth grade. She likes to draw, like me, but her main love is reading. She brings a book everywhere, even to art class. Since she also likes to write, she said she wants to make her own picture books one day.

Today Zeina was wearing a sky-blue hijab and had on pretty, robin's-egg-blue flats to match. She usually wasn't as adventurous as I am—which was probably a good thing—but she was still very stylish.

"Your outfit today is so cute!" I said. "I meant to tell you at lunch today but didn't get a chance to comment on it earlier."

Zeina beamed. "Thanks!"

When we walked into the art classroom, there was a big poster on the whiteboard at the front. It had the words

"Starscape Young Artists' Program" written in fancy cursive letters and had a picture of a big, fancy brick stone campus that looked like an Ivy League school. In front of the building were smiling kids painting on easels beneath a grove of willow trees. They looked so happy, like they were having the best time in the world.

Everyone was gathered in front of the poster, chatting excitedly about it. Ms. Williams, the art teacher, was nowhere to be seen. I guessed she was in the bathroom or something.

Zeina and I walked around the crowd of kids to sit down at the table with our other best friend, Carolina. Carolina had her head down, and I knew she was playing her Nintendo Switch since Ms. Williams was nowhere to be seen. Carolina loves playing video games and draws cool fan art of her favorite characters. She said she's still deciding on whether she wants to be an astronaut or a video game designer . . . or both! She moved to Bluebonnet at the beginning of fourth grade, but since then the three of us have been as thick as thieves.

"What's that about?" I asked, pointing at the poster.

Without looking up, Carolina replied, "Starscape! It's a prestigious summer art camp on the East Coast. Apparently, they have world-renowned teachers. An artist for one of my favorite video games is teaching this year! And so are famous graphic novelists and other artists."

Zeina and I both perked up. I took my phone out of my pocket and looked up more information about Starscape. Carolina was right. There were a bunch of cool people on the instructor list. I even spotted Christiana Moon, my favorite graphic novelist. I didn't know what I would do if I met Christiana in person, but this was my chance to get advice from the very best. She was Korean American too. Maybe she could help me figure out how to convince my parents to let me pursue art!

The bell rang then, and Ms. Williams rushed into class. Her curly brown hair looked even more frazzled than usual, and her warm dark eyes softened behind her bright red glasses when she saw us all staring at the poster.

"Okay, my artists!" she exclaimed, clapping her hands. "I'm happy to see so many of you excited about this camp, but please get into your seats so we can get started!"

When we all got settled down, she continued. "Before we begin today's class, I want to tell everyone all about Starscape. It's a summer camp that lasts for a month in a prestigious art school in the country. The location changes every year, and this year it'll be hosted by NYU! This will be our seventh year sending kids to this camp. Previous participants later got into many great art colleges, like RISD and Tisch!"

Tisch was my *dream* school, since that's the college Christiana went to. Starscape was also in NYC—and even hosted by NYU this year!—so it seemed like the perfect first step to reach my goal. I really hoped I could get into the camp.

In class later, we were working on our still-life paintings when Ms. Williams came over to inspect our work. She looked at all our artwork with an impressed smile on her face.

"Good job, ladies," she said. "I can always rely on you three to produce amazing work. Are any of you considering applying to Starscape?"

I nodded quickly. "Definitely! I want to go."

Zeina frowned. "I want to go too, but I don't know. I read the poster, and it's super expensive. My parents already pay for my oldest sister's college tuition, and my other sister is going to start next fall."

Ms. Williams winced. "That *is* quite the predicament. Especially since the cost of college is rising so much every year."

Carolina sighed. "My parents probably won't let me go, either. Especially not with the baby on the way. Apparently, babies are expensive. And a lot of work."

Carolina's mom was pregnant with her baby sibling. We didn't know its gender yet, but we did know they were due sometime next year.

"Congratulations to your mother!" Ms. Williams said. "But, oh dear, yes, this seems like very rough timing all around."

Everyone looked at me, and I stared at the ground.

"My parents don't even know I want to be an artist," I said. "I doubt they'd let me go, even if we could somehow afford it."

Ms. Williams frowned. "Well, that's too bad. On the off chance any of you girls do end up being able to go, be sure to ask me for a teacher recommendation. I'd be more than happy to write a glowing letter for all three of you!"

"When do we have to apply by?" asked Carolina, scrutinizing the poster at the front of the room.

"Great question, Carolina," Ms. Williams replied. "All the materials are due by December, but it's a rolling admission process, which means that the sooner you apply, the sooner you'll know if you got in or not. You're allowed to submit the artwork you made in class or by yourselves in the last couple of years. If you do decide to create new art to supplement what you've already made, we still have two months until the final deadline."

"And when do we need to have the money by?" Zeina asked.

"Well, aside from the application fee, you don't have to pay anything unless you get into the program," explained Ms.

Williams. "After that, all other fees aren't due until March of next year."

After the teacher left, I turned to my friends. "We *have* to at least try asking our parents. There's no harm in just asking, right? This could really help us in the future if we get in! Even though things may not be ideal now, they might get better by March!"

My friends shrugged. Neither of them looked very hopeful.

"I guess," Zeina replied. "I'll keep you guys updated."

"Same here," Carolina said. "Let's all report back at lunch tomorrow."

"Sounds good." I nodded, clenching my fists in excitement.

My parents probably wouldn't let me go either, but I wanted to remain hopeful. This could be the opportunity of a lifetime!

Two

The only time I could talk about Starscape with my parents was during dinner. My parents ran a small Korean grocery store a few blocks away from our house, so in the mornings they were up early opening the shop, while in the evenings they were tired after their long days. No matter how busy things got, though, Mom came home to cook meals and Dad closed the store for thirty minutes every day so we could all have dinner together.

"Family time is important," Mom said once when I asked her why she cooked dinner almost every day instead of ordering pizza or getting takeout. "For many Korean families, dinner isn't just a meal. It's when families can talk to each other, and the delicious food we eat while having conversations is the cornerstone of everything. Besides, Dad can watch the store on his own while I cook! So I have plenty of time to prepare the meals."

Even though my parents *say* they want to have conversations with us, what actually ends up happening is Tommy talks the entire time about his day and my parents and me just listen to him. Tommy is nine, and he is very loud and super dramatic. He always gives us a play-by-play about what happened at his school. I know the names of all the kids in his class without having to step foot into Longhorn Elementary again, all thanks to Tommy.

Today he was talking about how one kid named James got into trouble because he pulled a girl's hair.

"He yanked Pippa's braid really hard! She cried, and the teacher was so mad!"

Tommy banged his spoon on his bowl, and a bit of stew flew into my face. I ignored it as best I could. If I got mad at Tommy now, I might miss my chance to tell my parents about Starscape!

Today's dinner was fresh and piping-hot kimchi stew with tasty side dishes like mini seafood pancakes and braised potatoes. At our house, we always eat Korean food for dinner. Even though I sometimes wish we could eat pepperoni pizza or get Whataburger, I *do* like Mom's cooking more than anything else. Her food is so comforting, like a warm hug at the end of a long day.

Dad frowned. "That was not very nice of your friend. Did James apologize?"

"Of course! The teacher made him. And he had to go sit in time-out."

Tommy went on and on about other things that happened to him during the school day, and it took all my self-control to not interrupt him and say, "Shush. It's my turn now!"

I had to wait for the perfect moment so I could tell my parents about the camp when they were in the best moods possible. If I cut off Tommy and rushed into it now, my parents would be too busy telling me not to be rude to pay attention to anything I was saying. Too late, and Dad would get up from the table, say to my mom, "That was a good meal. I ate well!" in Korean and rush out the door. He was always the first one to finish eating since he had to return to the store.

Currently, Dad had more than half his rice left in his bowl, so I still had a lot of time. But I was getting worried. Tommy wasn't even close to finishing, even though he was talking a million words per minute.

"And then in class we learned division, and it was sooo hard—I don't think I can do it by myself. The rules are too confusing, I don't understand what remainders are. Why do we need long division anyway when there are calculators now? I wish I didn't have to learn it. . . ."

Finally, after Dad ate his third-to-last spoonful of rice, I had enough. I waited until Tommy stopped to take a breath and said, "Umma, Appa, can I ask you something?"

Mom and Dad turned from Tommy to me. They both looked shocked that I'd said something. I almost never spoke up during meals, mostly because I didn't want to fight for my parents' attention.

"Yes, Ji-Young?" Dad asked, calling me by my Korean name. "What is it?"

I brought out the pamphlet for Starscape from under the table. I'd had it on my lap during the entire meal. "There's this art camp I want to go to this summer. Ms. Williams said a lot of the students from our school who went there ended up going to the best art colleges! And she said she'd write me an amazing recommendation. One of my favorite artists is teaching at the camp this year, so I *really* want to go."

Dad slowly took the pamphlet from me and read through it with a frown. He gave it to Mom, who did the same. They looked at each other and then at me.

"Gigi," Mom said in English. "This camp is very expensive."

My parents usually spoke Korean to me, but when it was something important they wanted to be sure I understood, they spoke in English.

"Yes," Dad said. "With this kind of money, you could go

to a more useful camp that is more worth the money. Like a robotics or coding camp! Your cousin Min-seo went to one last year and found it very helpful. It'll be a great investment for your future since scientists and engineers make a lot of money."

"But I don't want to be an engineer or a scientist," I said. "I don't even like math. Or science. I want to be an artist."

Mom scoffed. "Artists don't make money. Look at Yeji-imo. She is living check to check in New York City. She can't even afford to buy a house!"

My aunt Yeji was her little sister, the "strange," youngest one who, according to Mom, wasn't "normal" like Min-seo's mom, my other aunt. On the outside, Yeji-imo looked like a younger Mom, but Mom had lots of frown lines while Yeji-imo had lots of dimples from smiling so much. I'd only seen her in person two times, when my grandparents passed away and the entire family gathered in Korea for the funerals, but I saw plenty about her life on Instagram. I didn't have my own Instagram account yet, but I occasionally logged into Min-seo's to keep up with Yeji-imo's updates.

Unlike Mom, who never traveled, Yeji-imo was somewhere brand-new, like Paris or Tokyo, every time I checked her profile. My parents said she didn't have money, but it sure didn't seem like it. She was always smiling in the pictures I saw, and her stylish clothes were covered in paint splotches in a cool way. She also had over a *million* followers! She was famous and had a whole career, all because people liked and bought her art. Even though my parents thought her life wasn't great, to me it looked amazing. I wanted to be like her when I grew up.

"I want to go to robotics club!" Tommy suddenly said, bursting into the conversation. "Can I go to robotics club, Umma and Appa? *I* like math and science!"

Tommy's Korean name was Ji-hoon, but his nickname was Tommy. He picked it because he likes Thomas the Tank Engine. *That's* how much my brother likes science and math. I picked my American name too, but only because I saw a picture of Gigi Hadid on a magazine cover at Walmart once when I was little and thought her name was cool and pretty. I think naming yourself after a real-life person is more normal than naming yourself after a cartoon train, but maybe that's just me.

Dad smiled at Tommy. He said in Korean, "We're not one hundred percent sure if we can afford any type of summer camp for you two right now, but we'll see what we can do!"

I couldn't believe it. I got a "this camp is very expensive," while Tommy got a "we'll see what we can do!"

Then again, I didn't know why I was surprised. Tommy was

the youngest, and he was a boy, so he was always getting spoiled. Whenever he wanted something, my parents got it for him. One time, he asked for an entire Thomas the Tank Engine train set for Christmas, and Mom and Dad bought it for him, even though it was super expensive.

My parents also thought Tommy's hobbies were better than mine, just because he liked math and science and I didn't, so they paid more attention to him than they did to me. Whenever he wanted to talk about something, like a type of dinosaur or how a plane engine worked, they spent hours discussing it with him and looking things up on the Internet for him when they didn't know the answers to his questions. When I tried talking about superhero comics or my drawings, my parents just told me to go study.

Sometimes it felt like my parents had enough time and money for Tommy and not me.

I looked down at my dinner and didn't say anything else for the rest of the meal.

Later that night, I was drawing in my sketchbook. I always drew when I felt sad like I was tonight. It helped me forget about the bad things in life.

I was drawing a picture of a Meteor Girl flying between the skyscrapers of NYC when there was a knock on my door.

"Ji-young?" It was Dad.

"Yeah?" I quickly hid my sketchbook in its usual place in my desk drawer and didn't turn around. I was still mad about what happened at dinner. And I didn't want my parents to see my art since they were bound to just ask me why I was drawing instead of studying.

"Are you done with your homework?" Dad asked when he came into my room.

"Yeah," I said again. "I finished it in study hall."

"Good. Tommy needs help with his homework. Normally, your mom and I can help him, but his word problems today are too hard for us. Can you go help?"

I didn't want to help Tommy, but through the open door, I could hear the frustrated groans coming from his room.

"Why is long division so hard!" he was saying.

I heard Mom speaking softly in Korean, but she sounded confused too. I was still pretty angry at my parents, but it really did sound like they needed my help. Since they came to the United States as grown-ups, English was hard for them sometimes.

"Okay," I said with a sigh. I went to Tommy's room.

My brother's desk was covered with crumpled-up balls of paper that had endless lines of long division. Mom looked tired, and Tommy was crying.

I frowned. Sure, I thought my little brother was annoying 99 percent of the time, but that didn't mean I liked to see him cry.

"I got this, Umma," I said in Korean. "You should go rest."

"Thank you, Ji-young," she said.

After Mom left, I looked over at Tommy's homework. My parents and my brother had managed to do most of the questions, with the exception of the five word problems at the very end of the sheet. I glanced over them. Math wasn't my best subject, but luckily, I could understand what to do.

"Scoot over," I told Tommy. He wiped his eyes and did what I said.

"So, what you do is," I said. "When it says 'divided by' something, you put that outside the division sign. Or when it says, 'split into groups of . . .' you have to be careful to see what is being divided by what and set up the equation on your own first, and then you can do the math like a normal long division question."

Tommy's mouth dropped open in a big O. "Is that all?"

"Yup!"

We tried doing a problem together. Tommy was confused at first, but toward the end, he was able to work it out himself. It didn't take him long to finish the rest of his homework after that.

"Wow, that was easier than I thought," he said. "You're a

good teacher, Noona. You're better than me at math!"

Noona was the Korean word that boys used for big sister. Since Tommy was my only little brother, he was the only person who called me Noona. It was a common Korean word, but whenever Tommy said it, it felt like a special name that he had just for me.

I shook my head. "I can only do this because this worksheet is for third graders. Math is my worst subject at school. You'll probably get a lot better at me soon. I'd much rather do social studies."

"Oh, really?" Tommy asked, his eyes wide with surprise. "I love math, and it's my favorite, even though I can't do some of the problems yet! I hate social studies and English. They're so hard! I don't know how you like them!"

And that's when I got the best idea ever.

Just because my parents couldn't pay for Starscape didn't mean I couldn't go. There were a lot of ways to make money. Like my brother and me, my friends and I were each good at different subjects. Besides art, I was good at history, Carolina was good at math and science, and Zeina was good at English.

We could start a tutoring club and raise money for ourselves!

That night I couldn't sleep. I was too excited by my idea. Lunchtime tomorrow couldn't come fast enough!

Three

The next day at lunch, Carolina and Zeina told me that their parents also said no to the camp. "It's okay," I said. "Because I have a great idea. Let's form a tutoring club!"

I pumped my fists in the air with excitement. Today I was wearing a denim jacket over my bright orange dress, along with white lace-up boots that made me feel way more confident than usual. And I really needed the energy, too, because my friends didn't seem all that happy with my idea.

"A tutoring club?" Zeina asked, wrinkling her nose. "Why?"

"So we can raise money for the camp ourselves!" I exclaimed. I was talking so fast with excitement that I reminded myself of Tommy at last night's dinner. "Think about it. We only need to apply by December, right? But we have until March to raise money to go. Tutoring is the perfect business opportunity for us! Besides art, we're all good at different things in school. I'm good at history; Carolina, you're like a math and science *genius*; and, Zeina, no one can write better essays in English class! We can use the local library as a tutoring center since it's within walking distance from our neighborhood and close to the school, too. We can help our little siblings' friends and other people from our school."

"I guess there's no harm in trying it out," Carolina said with a shrug. "And it's not like we're doing something bad. We'll be helping people."

"Yeah!" I said. "Plus, it'll be a lot of fun. We'll get to hang out after school every day."

Just the idea of getting to see my friends after school every day made me smile. It was going to be so awesome!

"I've never taught anything before. . . ." Zeina said. "I don't even have younger siblings, so I've never had to help them out with homework. I've babysat for the neighborhood aunties, but that's pretty much it."

"Come to think of it, I've never taught anyone anything, either," Carolina added. "I've only babysat too. Gigi, I think you're the only one with actual tutoring experience."

This could be a problem, but I hoped my friends would

be able to learn how to tutor kids quickly. It couldn't be that hard, right? It was like babysitting, but you just had to teach them things.

"I'm sure you two will be able to get the hang of it," I said. "I tutor Tommy all the time, and it's not very hard."

"Okay," Zeina said, scratching her head. "If we're going to have our own business, we'll need a cool, classic name to catch people's attention. Like the Babysitters' Club! What should we call ourselves?"

"How about the Renaissance Society?" Carolina asked.

"The *what*?" exclaimed Zeina and me.

"The Renaissance Society!" Carolina said again. "The Renaissance was a period in Europe when a bunch of cool inventions and art were made. We're all artists and we're good at different things, like Zeina is with English and me with science, so why don't we name ourselves after the Renaissance?"

"That's a cool reason," said Zeina. "But isn't the name too hard? How are the little kids going to say that? We can barely say it ourselves."

Carolina frowned. "Okay, then what else should we call it?"

We brainstormed until the end of lunch, when I suddenly had a burst of inspiration.

"How about the Ace Squad?" I asked. "The name's easy enough for little kids to say, and we're all aces at our own subjects."

"And we can help people ace their tests!" Zeina exclaimed. "Sounds great, Gigi!"

Carolina grimaced. "I think it sounds a little corny, but if you two like it . . . that's fine by me."

Zeina looked from Carolina to me and then back again with a nervous expression on her face. I was uneasy about Carolina, too, but what could we do? Zeina agreed with me that the Ace Squad was the better name.

"Okay, that settles it," I finally said. "We're officially the Ace Squad!"

Since art was the class we all had together, we decided to start spreading the word about the Ace Squad there first. During lunchtime, we met at the library to make flyers that we could pass out to our classmates.

"What can we say to convince people to come to us for help?" Zeina wondered out loud as we stared at the blank Word document.

I thought about tutoring Tommy and how I could help him better than anyone my parents knew.

"Well, first of all, the three of us all go to this school. And we went to Longhorn Elementary, too. So we know what all the teachers and classes are like. That's better than any adult tutor already, right?"

"That's so true!" replied Zeina. She turned back to the computer and typed, "Need homework help from someone who's actually in or has been in your classes? Call the Ace Squad today!"

"Can we add that people can also text us?" Carolina asked. "I mean, we all have smartphones, right? And who even makes phone calls these days, besides old people?"

"That's so true!" I said.

Zeina nodded and added, "Or text" after "Call" on the poster.

Carolina grinned. She looked happy that we agreed with her.

We included some additional details, like where to meet—at the local library—and when the sessions were—every day after school. As a finishing touch, we all added our favorite memes at the bottom of the poster, to grab people's attention. I picked the one with the crying lady screaming at the cat. It was an old meme, but it was a classic.

We were printing out the flyers when Paul Kim Wiley walked into the library. He looked frazzled, and his hair was tousled in a cute way. He scanned the room, looking for an empty table. When he glanced in our direction, I gave him a quick wave before I could chicken out. He waved back, a brief smile flashing on his face as he rushed over to an empty table he spotted on the far side of the room.

"He is so cute," Carolina said. It took me a moment to realize she was talking about Paul. "I know most of the popular guys aren't worth the hype, but Paul really is. I keep hearing about how nice he is."

Carolina's voice was all hushed and excited, a tone I'd never heard her use to talk about a real person before. Usually when Carolina talked like this, she was talking about a cool video game character or her favorite invention.

Does Carolina have a crush on Paul too? I wondered. But I knew I shouldn't be surprised. Most of the girls in the school did, including me.

"Yeah, he's pretty nice," I replied. "He's in my choir class, and I had Korean school with him when we were little."

Zeina gasped, joining in on our conversation. "You used to know Paul Kim Wiley as a kid, and you never told us?"

I shrugged. "It never came up."

It felt weird to be talking to my friends about Paul. Even though I *knew* he was one of the most popular guys in my school, I've always kept my thoughts and feelings about him private.

I looked back at Paul, who was deeply focused on a worksheet. He had a big frown on his face. It'd been a while since I'd seen him this frustrated about something.

"Hey, should we ask Paul if he wants tutoring?" Zeina joked.

"No!" Carolina and I both yelled at the same time. Just the thought of going up to him to ask made my heart leap inside my chest. And from the wide-eyed look in Carolina's eyes, I could tell she felt exactly the same way.

Zeina laughed and said, "I was just kidding. Although honestly there would be no harm in asking him, right? We need all the students we can get!"

"Uh, *yes*, there would," I said. "I would have to actually talk to him. The last time I did that, I thought I was going to combust."

My friends and I giggled.

"Okay, so maybe we ask Paul as a last resort," Zeina amended. "Like, if no one else on the entire planet wants tutoring. I think the flyers are done printing, by the way. Let's all grab a bunch and pass them out in art class."

When sixth period finally came along, we showed the flyers to Ms. Williams before we passed them out.

"Carolina, Zeina, and I are trying to raise money to go to Starscape," I said. "Is it okay if we pass these out at the end of class, during independent work time?"

Ms. Williams looked over the posters and clapped her hands. "Fabulous initiative, girls! And you sure can. You three are all such hard workers that I trust you to get your work done on time. Just be sure to be respectful to your classmates. You don't want to accidentally startle someone and cause them to mess up their masterpieces!"

"Got it and will do," Carolina replied. "Thanks, Ms. Williams!"

"Oh, also, why don't you leave one up on the whiteboard so people from my other periods can see it too?" added the art teacher. "I'm sure it can be helpful to other students, and not just the ones in this period."

"Wow, thanks, Ms. Williams!" I exclaimed.

Later in class, during independent work time, Carolina, Zeina, and I split up so we could cover all the tables in the art room. Like Ms. Williams warned, we were extra careful to only talk to people when it seemed like they were at a natural stopping point. I would be really annoyed if someone interrupted *me* while I was in the middle of a paint stroke!

The first person I talked to was Caleb Santiago, who sat at the table next to me and my friends. Caleb was always complaining about how hard math was, so I knew he was the perfect potential student! Since he was also Paul's friend, some part of me hoped he would tell Paul about our club too. So I didn't have to myself.

I waited until he'd finished painting the corner of his

canvas before I said, "Psst, hey, Caleb! Carolina, Zeina, and I are starting a tutoring club if you still need help with math."

Caleb took the poster from my hands and stared at it.

"Help with math? From you?" he asked with a grin. "You're joking, right? Aren't you bad at math too? I hear you complaining to your friends about it all the time."

I rolled my eyes. "Don't worry. I'm going to be teaching history. Carolina is our math teacher! She always gets As. Anyway, we're trying to raise money so we can go to Starscape. So feel free to reach out if you need help, okay? With anything."

"Cool," Caleb said. "Good luck!"

"Thanks!"

Besides Caleb, though, I didn't have much luck recruiting anyone. The other people I talked to either didn't seem interested or were too busy working on their projects to talk with me. I regrouped with Carolina and Zeina in the last five minutes of class.

"I could barely talk to anyone!" Zeina exclaimed. "How about you guys?"

"Same here," Carolina said. "Everyone I did talk to said they were already getting tutored by someone else. I think we need another strategy."

Before I could respond, the bell rang, and everyone

around us started rushing out of the classroom.

"Let's brainstorm ideas tomorrow!" I said as my friends and I headed out, too. "We got this!"

In reality, I wasn't sure if we "got" anything. But I put on a brave face for my friends as we headed to our next classes.

four

It took us the entire lunch period, but by the end of it, my friends and I managed to come up with different ideas on how we could spread the word about the Ace Squad in various ways. Carolina said she'd ask her gamer friends at school while Zeina said she could ask her book club friends. Meanwhile, since I was the only one with a little sibling—for now anyway—we decided I could ask Tommy and—after making him swear he won't tell our parents—get him to tell his many, *many* friends about our tutoring club.

When I told Tommy about the Ace Squad after school, he folded his arms in front of him.

"Hmph," he said. "What do I get from all this? This just sounds like another chore!"

"I'll help you out with your schoolwork for free!" I replied.

"But you already do that now!"

I raised my eyebrows. "I won't once we start this club!"

Tommy gasped. "You wouldn't! Noona, that's so mean!"

I crossed my arms and kept going. "Do you *really* want to spend your Lunar New Year money on tutoring when you can spend it on a new toy train or a Lego set?"

Tommy quickly shook his head. "Okay, okay! I'll tell my friends about your club! And I won't tell Mom and Dad."

He held out a pinkie, and we made a pinkie promise. I had to try my hardest to keep a straight face. My little brother was too cute sometimes; it was hard not to smile.

Toward the end of the week, we didn't have many kids signed up for classes, but we had enough that everyone was teaching one class every day. There were also a lot of students who said they needed help with other stuff, like French and speech and debate.

"I could ask my friend Emma if she wants to join the squad," said Carolina. "She's amazing at speech and debate, French, and other stuff too!"

I never had any classes with Emma Chen, so I didn't know her, but I saw her a couple of times at lunch and during Carolina's birthday parties. Emma was Taiwanese and was always stylish, like Zeina. But unlike Zeina and me, she wore things our parents would never let us wear, like pink short-shorts and black miniskirts. She also wore thick eyeliner that made her look like she was mad all the time.

Carolina said she was actually really nice, but I was still worried. A large part of why I wanted to do this club was so I could spend more time with my friends. Having a stranger like Emma join us made me nervous. I wasn't good at making new friends, and besides Carolina and Zeina, I didn't normally talk to anyone at school.

In the end, I asked Carolina to formally introduce Emma to us so we could all see how she would fit into our squad. The club wasn't all mine, after all, so my friends should have a say in whether they wanted Emma to have a part in this too.

On Friday, Carolina invited Emma to sit with us at our table during lunch.

Emma was wearing all black and had on a beret, like she'd just gotten off a plane from Paris. Her outfit was cool, but her dark kohl eyeliner made her look like a scary raccoon.

When she sat down next to me, she was chewing bright pink bubble gum. She popped it and said, "Hey," to my friends and me.

"Hi!" I said. My voice came out louder than usual. I was nervous already! But then I remembered, this was *our* club. I had nothing to be anxious about.

I cleared my throat and asked, "So, why do you want to join the Ace Squad?"

Emma shrugged. "Well, my mom cut my allowance after I got caught on a date with a boy. . . ."

Zeina gasped, and I tried my hardest not to. If that ever happened to me, I was pretty sure my parents would ground me for life.

"And I need money so I can buy more clothes so I can make more designs. Carolina also told me about Starscape, so I looked it up and saw that they have a fashion design category! So it'd be cool if I could raise enough money to go too. My parents *technically* can afford to send me to the camp, but they probably won't pay for it since they want me to go to an 'academic' camp."

I got really excited. Emma was into fashion, too! And I could totally relate to what she said about her parents not wanting her to go to an artsy camp.

"Same here!" I said. "Well, the parents wanting me to go to an 'academic' camp part, that is. Who is your favorite designer?"

"Alexander McQueen!" Emma exclaimed. The scary expression on her face instantly disappeared, and she looked as excited as I felt. "He's not going to be at the camp, of course, rest in peace. But he was such a *visionary*!"

"I love his designs!" I replied. "They're so creative."

Emma and I grinned at each other. Could this be the beginning of a new friendship?

Not wanting to get ahead of myself, I moved on to the next question. "Do you have any experience teaching kids or people our age?"

"Kind of," Emma replied sheepishly. "I volunteer at my Chinese school on Saturdays. There's an adult teacher there, but I help little kids whenever they don't understand what the teacher is saying."

I nodded. That was more experience than most of us had, so I was impressed.

I turned to my friends. "Do y'all have any questions for Emma?"

By "y'all," I mostly meant Zeina, since Carolina was already friends with Emma, but Carolina surprised me by asking Emma, "What's your availability like during the week?"

"On Fridays I'm busy because I have dance class, and on Saturdays I'm pretty busy with Chinese school," replied Emma. "But I'm free any other day on weekdays. And maybe some Sundays if necessary."

No one had any more questions after that, so after a while, Emma asked, "So . . . am I in?"

She looked nervous this time, and even bit her lip. She definitely seemed way less intimidating than before.

"I don't have any more questions," I finally said. "Zeina, you didn't ask any. Is there anything you want to ask Emma?"

Zeina startled and said, "I do, but it's not about the squad."

I shrugged. "It's okay. Go ahead and ask it."

With a shy smile, Zeina asked, "Emma, where did you get that shirt?"

We all burst out laughing. Emma grinned and told Zeina she got her cute black blouse at Forever 21, and suddenly it was like a floodgate had broken loose. Any remaining nerves melted away, and we were soon chatting away about clothes, games, and school stuff like we'd all been friends for a long time.

I'd had my doubts about Emma, but I was glad I was wrong. And best of all, now we had a full roster of tutors ready for next week. The Ace Squad was really happening!

Five

Our first official meeting of the Ace Squad was the following Sunday at Zeina's house. There was no way we could have the meeting at my house, and we didn't want to disturb Carolina's mom since she needed a lot of rest. And neither Zeina nor I knew where Emma lived, so Zeina's was the best option.

On Sundays my parents didn't open the store until the afternoon since our family went to Korean church in the morning. When I told Mom that I was going to Zeina's house after church, she didn't even look up from where she was cooking in the kitchen.

"Okay. Be back in time for dinner!" she said before I closed the door.

I rushed over to the house next to ours. Even though I'd been going over to Zeina's house since as far back as I could remember, visiting her always made my head kind of hurt because her house looked almost exactly like ours except for a few differences. Our houses were based on the same model, but the layout was flipped, so instead of the kitchen being left of the living room, the living room was the one on the left. The colors were different too, so although our houses had the same bricks on the outside, hers was a lighter color than ours.

"Oh, hey, Gigi," Zeina's older sister, Aya, said as she opened the door. She pushed her glasses up on her nose to peer down at me.

Aya was in high school and was very tall. She always looked stressed nowadays, and Zeina said it was because she was currently applying for colleges. Apparently senior year was really tough!

"Zeina and your other friends are already in Zeina's room," Aya continued. "Can you tell them to keep it down? I have my last SAT on Saturday, so I have to study."

I gulped. I was so glad I didn't have to worry about scary stuff like college apps or SATs yet. "Okay! Good luck."

"Thanks," Aya said with a grimace. She held the door open for me so I could come in.

Zeina's room was where Tommy's was in our house, except while Tommy's was full of Legos and toy trains, Zeina's was full of books, plants, and cozy candles. From picture books to classic romance novels, Zeina had every book I'd ever heard of. It was like Zeina's own little library!

When I came in, everyone looked up at me from where they were sitting on Huda's bed. Before Huda, Zeina's oldest sister, went off to college, this used to be the room she shared with Zeina. But now Zeina and I used Huda's bed as the "official hangout" spot, where we normally sat and lay about when we talked about random stuff.

I waved at Zeina, Carolina, and Emma, and they all waved back.

"Hi!" I whispered. "Aya told me to tell you guys to keep it down. She's studying for the SATs."

Zeina sighed quietly. "She's always studying for the SATs. I hope this one's the last time, though. She's so mean when she's stressed!"

"Does she know what she wants to study in college yet?" I asked as I plopped down in between Zeina and Carolina on the bed.

"Pre-med, just like Huda is doing now. And, of course, my parents are all for it. It's probably what they'll want me to do too."

Zeina sighed again, and Carolina and I looked at each other.

"Just because your parents want you to do something doesn't mean you have to do it!" Emma exclaimed. "I never do what my parents want me to do."

"It's just hard to go against the grain when your parents are both doctors and your two older sisters want to walk the same path, too," replied Zeina. "I mean, I wish I liked science too! But I just don't get it. Without Carolina's help, I probably wouldn't understand half the problem bank questions."

"I guess I'm lucky to be good at both the arts and sciences," Carolina said, almost apologetically.

Zeina shook her head. "It's nothing you should feel sorry about! It's awesome that you can do both. But yeah, anyway, we should get started on the club planning. I really want us to go to this camp! It'll be a good way for my parents to see I'm serious about art so they'll know it's not just some hobby for me."

Carolina nodded. "That's kind of why I want to go to Starscape, too," she replied. "My parents want me to go into science, and although I do like science, I also like video games, you know? No way they would give me money to go to a camp to learn how to make video games. I want to go and try it out so I can decide what I really want to do."

"I mean, you could always do both," Emma said with a shrug. "There's no reason you can't be an astronaut and make video games. Maybe you can design a game about space. Like the next Halo!"

Carolina giggled. "Maybe!"

She turned on her tablet to reveal the spreadsheet where we had our teaching schedule for the first week. Since we didn't want people to forget to show up after the weekend, we'd decided to have next Tuesday as our first day of tutoring.

"Okay," Carolina continued. "We should get down to business and talk about how we want to start things on our first day."

"Yes!" I replied. "Well, I was thinking we could each take one of the tables in the library's study area. Hopefully that can help keep the noise levels down, too. Since there will only be two people at each table."

Carolina opened her mouth like she was about to say something. But before she could, Zeina exclaimed, "That's a good idea, Gigi! And each session is going to be an hour, right? Is that going to be enough time to help people with their homework?"

"I think so!" I replied. "At least for the first session or so. Maybe we can have longer sessions later if we think it's necessary. Carolina, were you going to say something?"

Carolina blinked. "Oh, I was. But you guys already talked about it. We can move on to other stuff."

We talked more about the logistics of how Tuesday was going to work, and I tried to give my friends my best tutoring advice from the times I'd tutored Tommy.

"The most important thing is to be patient," I said. "Especially with the little kids. Even though you think something is easy, it doesn't mean it's easy for the other person. Tommy usually pays attention, but in the rare times he doesn't, I also like to do something fun, like doodle on the page! Kids really like it when you draw since it keeps things fun."

Zeina nodded, taking notes in her notebook. Emma and Carolina nodded too.

"Yeah, I'm definitely going to keep things interesting," Emma replied. "Luckily none of my subjects are boring."

Carolina groaned. "A lot of people hate math and science, so I might have my work cut out for me. But I'll do my best!"

Zeina and I shot Carolina a guilty grin. She smiled back at us.

By the end of our meeting, I had a pretty good feeling about everything.

"Okay!" I said. "So now all we have to do is send out reminders on Monday, and we'll be ready to go!"

I wanted to end our meeting in a cool way, but I didn't know what I could do. So in the end I put my hand out. "Okay, everyone, put your hands on mine. Let's do a cheer!"

My friends gave me a funny look.

"But this is exactly why I didn't join cheerleading!" Emma protested. But she put her hand on mine anyway. I grinned. From her tone, I could tell she was just trying to be funny and not mean.

When everyone's hands were stacked on mine in the middle, I said, "Let's go, Ace Squad!"

"Yeah!" exclaimed Zeina and Carolina.

"Go, sports!" Emma said.

Everyone laughed. I had a good feeling about the week ahead!

Six

All the confidence I felt during our meeting fizzled out into nothing when we showed up at the library on Tuesday afternoon for the first day of tutoring. I felt sick. It was strange, since I'd been so excited up until then. But for some reason, now I felt queasy. And my friends looked like they weren't doing any better.

I stared down at my outfit, hoping it would give me the same confidence I'd felt when I put it on this morning. Since today was our first day, I'd worn my most professional-looking white blouse, the one my mom had bought me for choir concerts. But instead of the boring black skirt I usually wore with it, I had on my electric-green pants, which usually gave me a jolt of energy when I wore them.

Right now, though, I felt neither professional nor energized. Instead, I felt like I was going to throw up!

Could we have all gotten a mysterious stomach flu from school? I hoped not. If we were sick, we would get all the people at the library sick, and it'd all be a huge disaster.

"Psst," I hissed at Carolina as we made our way to the tables in the group study area. "Come here!"

Carolina gave me a questioning look but did what I said anyway.

I put one hand on my forehead and put the other on Carolina's. Neither of our foreheads seemed that much hotter than the other.

"What are you doing?" Carolina asked.

"I'm trying to see if either of us has a fever," I replied. "Do you feel sick?"

She made a confused face at me. "No? Also, if both of us had a fever, wouldn't you not be able to tell? The forehead trick only works when one person isn't sick. Maybe I should have brought my thermometer."

Carolina had a point. I guess this was why she was good at science, and I wasn't.

"I'm sure we're all just nervous because it's the first day of tutoring," she continued. "We were fine in school today. The chances of us just spontaneously getting sick now are very low."

I sighed. "You're right."

I did feel really anxious. I wanted to go home, pull up my favorite webtoon on my phone, and read in bed.

"Should I be nervous?" Emma asked with a shrug. "I feel fine."

Emma looked so cool today with her maroon lipstick and cat-eye liner. Unlike the rest of us, she did seem like she wasn't anxious at all. I wished I could be cool like her and not so jittery. How was I going to be a good teacher if I was so nervous in the first place?

"It's okay to be nervous," Zeina said, matter-of-fact. "Or not nervous. Everyone has different responses to things. Let's try not to think about how we're feeling and more about the students we're seeing today so we can be prepared."

We all nodded. I tried to focus on what I knew about my student today.

Carly was one of Tommy's friends. But I'd only ever seen her at a few of his birthday parties. I didn't know much about her other than that she had long, curly brown hair and wore pink, boxy glasses. When I asked him over the weekend, Tommy told me she was nice. So at least there was that!

My friends and I each took a table. There were only five minutes left until our sessions started. As the club founder,

I felt like I had to say something. I stood up from my seat and made eye contact with each of my friends, one by one. "Okay, guys, here we go. Only five minutes left! I know it's kind of scary, but we can do it! We each only have one kid today. How bad can it be?"

My friends nodded. We braced ourselves as we waited for people to trickle in.

The first student to arrive was Emma's. He was a sixth grader named Benny who was in his soccer uniform.

"I'm going to soccer practice after this," he explained when Emma asked him why he was wearing his uniform.

Next, Zeina's student, one of Carolina's gamer friends, arrived, and then Carolina's. Soon everyone had their student except me!

I checked the time. It was ten minutes past four. Where was Carly?

The more time passed, the more jittery I got. Just as I was about to pack up my things and leave, Carly shuffled into the library at exactly 4:30 p.m. She was thirty minutes late!

And that wasn't all. Carly's hair was all tangled up, and her Captain Marvel T-shirt was rumpled like she'd just woken up from a nap. As she sat down, her mouth opened into a big yawn.

"Sorry!" Carly said. "I forgot I had this."

I didn't want to be the mean tutor in the very first lesson, so I just smiled and said, "That's okay! What do you want to work on today?"

Carly sighed and looked at the clock, as if she already didn't want to be there. "Just some boring history stuff."

I wondered if Tommy had been wrong when he said Carly was nice. What if Carly was only nice to Tommy because they were friends?

I tried my best to keep my smile. But my cheek muscles were starting to hurt.

"Can you take out your homework?" I asked. "Tommy said you told him you need help."

"It's just so boring!" Carly whined. She took her history book out of her backpack and slammed it onto the table. "The only reason I came here is because my mom said I had to pass history if I wanted to watch the new Avengers movie."

My cheeks burned up with frustration. I glanced around, hoping no one else was staring at us. But fortunately—or unfortunately—it looked like my friends had their hands full with their own students. Carolina's student, one of Tommy's other friends, kept playing with a handful of slime, while Zeina's student kept trying to play games on his phone. Meanwhile, Benny, Emma's student, was yelling at her! From the schedule, I knew Benny was here to practice speech and debate with her, but his reaction seemed way too extreme.

Was this all a big mistake? What if we were in over our heads?

I shook my head. Even if this was a mistake, it was too late to do anything about it now. It wasn't like we could stop the sessions in the thick of things. My only option was to trust my friends to take care of their students while I did my best with mine.

I took a deep breath and then remembered what Carly had said about wanting to see the new Avengers movie. Maybe I could use that somehow! I loved superhero comics too.

I looked at Carly's worksheet. It looked easy since it was just asking about the different Founding Fathers and who did what. All Carly had to do was read the book and fill out the worksheet. But I guess even that was hard when you were too bored to stay focused.

"History isn't boring," I said as I got out a piece of paper and a pencil from my backpack. "If you think about it, it's like one long superhero movie!"

Carly gave me a quizzical look and watched carefully as I drew the Founding Fathers one by one, starting with George Washington.

"What are you doing?" Carly asked. For the first time since

she got there, she seemed curious and not angry.

"I'm drawing the Founding Fathers!" I said. "I love superheroes, too, and for me, drawing out things like this helps me study."

I made sure to give George Washington a fancy white wig and a square jaw. I remembered from when our class learned about the presidents in fourth grade that Washington always frowned in his pictures because he had bad teeth.

"Wow, that looks just like Washington!" Carly said. "You're so good at drawing."

I beamed. "Thanks! What do you know about George Washington? You can look at the book if you want!"

Carly didn't grab the book yet, and instead bit her lip and said, "Well, he was the first president."

"Yup!"

"He led the American soldiers to victory against the British."

"That's right! You're on a roll."

To make things fun, I gave Washington big muscles and a cape.

Carly giggled. "He looks like a superhero!"

"That's the point! Can you think of anything else to add for Washington? You can try looking in the book for more ideas."

Carly eagerly opened the book. But when she started reading, she looked lost, as if this was the first time she'd read it. I really hoped it wasn't!

"Ummm," she said. "Oh, I know! George Washington is important because people wanted him to be the king, but he said no! And it's because of him that our presidents today have only two terms!"

"You're right!" I put a crown below Washington's feet, so it looked like he was stomping on it.

"Let's do John Adams next!" Carly exclaimed before I could even finish working on Washington. I grinned. She was so excited about her homework now! It was a complete 180-degree change from how she was before.

We were halfway into writing John Adams's profile when there was a loud crash.

Carly and I looked up to see Benny standing with his chair on the ground behind him.

"You're wrong!" he said. "School uniforms are stupid! Why would anyone want to go to a school with uniforms?"

"Shh, calm down!" Emma hissed. "In debate, there is no right or wrong! It's all just a matter of proving your point."

Even though Emma had seemed so calm before, she was definitely not now. She shot me a panicked look, but before I could help, a lady asked, "What is going on here?"

Everyone turned around to see Ms. Kensington, the librarian. She looked super annoyed and had her arms crossed in front of her chest.

"This is a quiet studying area. I'm going to have to ask you two to leave, as you're disrupting the other patrons."

My other friends and I shot each other panicked looks. How was Emma going to finish her teaching session now?

But Emma didn't look fazed in the slightest. "Fine, we'll go sit outside. Come on, Benny. Grab your things."

Benny looked unsure, but he did what Emma said. I gulped. I hoped they could still have a good session!

It took a while for everyone to refocus after that. But soon enough Carly and I got through all the Founding Fathers together. After that, it took her only five minutes to fill out the worksheet by herself!

"Wow, that was so easy!" Carly exclaimed. "Thanks a lot!"

"No problem!" I replied. I was so happy I could help her that I couldn't stop smiling.

Since Carly finished her homework so quickly, we had fifteen minutes to spare, so I let her go home early.

"This was fun," she said on her way out. "I'm definitely going to come back for another session."

"Great!" I beamed. My heart felt a thousand times lighter. "See you later, then!"

"See you!"

After she left, I spent the rest of the time helping Zeina and Carolina with their students. Luckily, they only needed a tiny bit of assistance, and my friends eventually seemed to get the hang of things, just like I did with Carly.

When our sessions were over, the three of us gathered our things and rushed out of the library. We were all worried about Emma!

But when we went outside, we found Emma and Benny laughing about something. They both gave us a friendly wave when we reached them.

"Oh, hey, guys!" Emma said.

"Are you and Benny okay?" I asked. "We were so worried when you guys got kicked out!"

"We're fine," Emma replied. "Things were a little heated at first, but that's just what happens in debate sometimes. We had a lot of fun in the end, though. Right, Benny?"

He nodded. "Yup! It was fun and I learned a lot, even though I still think I'm right!"

Everyone laughed.

My friends and I gave each other tired smiles. Even though things didn't work out exactly the way we'd thought they would, we'd all survived our first day of tutoring!

When I came back home, my parents were still at the store. Tommy wasn't home, either. He was probably over at one of his friends' houses.

After I finished my homework, I opened my sketchbook. I flipped to a new page and started sketching the Founding Father superheroes that I'd drawn earlier for Carly. I'd let her keep the drawings I did at the library so she could use them to study, but I wanted to have my own copies of them to commemorate the club's successful first day of tutoring. I hadn't been sure things would all work out today, but I was so glad they did! I was excited for future sessions of the Ace Squad.

After I finished drawing the Founding Fathers, I went on Instagram using Min-seo's account.

Like I always did, I typed "yeji_kim_art," Yeji-imo's username, into the search bar.

She'd posted three pictures since the last time I logged in, the most recent being of herself sitting on the steps in front of the Met. She had on a blue beret and a black trench coat that looked so cool! Below the picture, the caption just read, *Sundays at the Met.* Short and sweet.

I clutched my phone tightly and went back to my sketchbook. This time I drew a panel of Meteor Girl standing on the steps of the Met.

Next summer my friends and I could go to NYC in real life. I could attend Christiana Moon's class and learn how to draw comics from the very best. Zeina could prove to her parents that she was serious about becoming an illustrator, Carolina could figure out if she wants to be a video game designer, and Emma could study in the fashion capital of the United States.

We could do so much at Starscape! We only had to keep having good tutoring sessions with the kids so we could raise enough money to go.

New York, I thought. *I'll be there soon!*

Seven

The rest of the week was pretty boring up until Thursday afternoon, when Mr. Martin held auditions for the solo parts in choir class. I didn't try out, of course, but I liked watching other people audition. Especially Paul.

Paul was one of the only guys to audition, and he looked nervous. At first his voice was shaky, and even all the way from where I was sitting at the back of the class, I could see the sweat dripping down his forehead.

"Go, Paul!" said a girl at the front. A few other kids joined in, and I did too. Paul looked around, and his eyes met mine. He smiled, and he was so cute I had to look away.

A lot more confident than he was before, Paul sang. I didn't know much about music, but even I could tell he was *amazing.* His voice was soft and warm, and when I briefly closed my eyes, I could picture sunlight streaming in through a window on an otherwise cloudy day. Since Mr. Martin had his back turned toward the rest of us, I got out my sketchbook and started drawing.

I couldn't think of a good name for the character I was drawing yet, but for now I called him Choir Boy. Choir Boy's superpowers were his heart of gold and his beautiful voice, which was so awesome that it made everyone and everything instantly happy. It even made plants sprout from the ground!

I worked on a panel with Meteor Girl and Choir Boy until the bell rang and it was time to go to our next class.

I was in a good mood for the rest of the day and was even humming the song Paul had sung as I headed to the library after school. Since the rest of the week had been peaceful, I was feeling confident about today's session. It was going to be like any other day this week. Or so I thought.

We had twins scheduled for the same hour block today, Kevin and Felicity. They were in fourth grade, and Felicity was scheduled to study English with Zeina while Kevin was learning history with me. Kevin was one of Tommy's best friends, so I knew him pretty well, but I didn't know much about Felicity.

From the moment they walked in this afternoon, though,

I had a very bad feeling. When he was playing with Tommy, Kevin always seemed so happy, but today he stomped into the library, his fists stuffed into his pockets and a big frown on his face. Felicity looked angry too, and she held her nose up high like she was pretending Kevin didn't exist.

Luckily, Zeina and I were sitting on opposite sides of the study area today. That was probably enough to stop anything disastrous from happening. Or so I thought.

"Kevin, over here!" I waved him over to my table.

"Felicity, hi!" exclaimed Zeina from where she was sitting. She raised her hand and gave Felicity a big wave since she was sitting farther away than I was.

The other students trickled in, and when the sessions began, everyone started talking . . . except the twins.

"Um, is everything okay?" I asked Kevin.

He slammed his fists onto the table, making me jump. "No! Because *someone* broke my Nintendo Switch when I'd just gotten it!"

From across the room, Felicity abruptly stood up so her chair clattered onto the ground. "One, it was *our* Switch. And two, you're the one who dropped it when you handed it to me!"

"Did not!"

"Did too!"

Before I or any one of my friends could react, Felicity rushed over to Kevin, and they started rolling around on the ground, trying to hit each other!

Emma buried her face in her hands, while the rest of us looked on with our mouths wide open. Everything had happened so fast!

Even though it felt like I was having an out-of-body experience, I tried to get between the twins.

But it was too late. Before I could separate them, Ms. Kensington rushed over and hissed at us, "*What* is going on here? I'm going to have to ask you two to leave."

Things had somehow become way worse than they ever were on Monday. How had things gotten this bad so quickly?

As the leader of the Ace Squad, I felt like I had to do something. I held out my hands as I approached Ms. Kensington so she knew I came in peace.

"Ms. Kensington, please let them stay! They just had a disagreement about something on the way to the library. We'll be quiet from now on, we promise! I—"

"This place sucks!" Kevin interrupted me.

We all stared in shock as he stomped out the library doors.

Ms. Kensington was the first to recover.

"Well," she said with a harumph. She gestured at the study area. "Out of respect for the other patrons in the library, there is strictly no talking at all allowed in this area today. Please be silent for the rest of the day or leave."

My friends and I shot frantic looks at each other. We couldn't teach if we couldn't talk!

Even though alarm bells went off in my head, I did the only thing I could think of doing at that moment. I started packing up my bag.

"Come on, guys," I said. "Let's go out to the back. Sorry, Ms. Kensington. We'll be better next time."

From the many times I'd ridden my bike with Zeina to the library, I knew that the back area had a nice garden with a small lake and benches where people could sit and read books. I wasn't entirely sure there would be enough seats for everyone, but it was better than nothing.

"I'll fetch Kevin and meet up with you and everyone else in the back area," I told Zeina.

She nodded, and I said to Felicity, "Come on, let's go get your brother."

The two of us caught up with Kevin at the front of the library. His face was still red from earlier, but he looked more embarrassed than mad.

"Sorry," he mumbled to me. "I didn't mean for things to get so bad."

"Yeah," said Felicity. "I'm sorry, too. Maybe Kevin and I

should have waited until after tutoring to fight. It wasn't fair for everyone else."

I couldn't believe my ears. After all the chaos they caused inside the library, the twins were actually agreeing on something now! It was too bad this couldn't have happened earlier.

It would have been so easy to get mad at the siblings for ruining today's session. After all, what they did *wasn't* fair, just like Felicity had said. But this was one of those cases where the easiest thing to do wasn't the right one. If I was mean and didn't accept the twins' apology, that would ruin the squad's reputation for sure. Plus, they were clearly sorry about what happened.

I thought about how, on Monday, Emma and her student, Benny, were still able to have a good session even after they got kicked out. Maybe not all hope was lost after all.

"It's okay," I finally said. "We still have a lot of time left with this session, so let's try not to waste any more time."

I led the siblings to the back of the library, where thankfully, there were just enough seats for everyone. Ducks swam across the lake, and the fountain in the middle burbled in a calming way. We were all quiet, taking everything in.

After all the stress back in the library, I was grateful for this moment of peace. I liked being out here in nature. Watching the ducks was peaceful, and I loved seeing people walk by the library with their dogs.

"Look, a puppy!" Kevin exclaimed, pointing in the direction where I'd been looking.

Everyone gasped and exclaimed, "Awww!" when they saw the golden retriever puppy walking by with its owner.

My friends and I exchanged smiles. Somehow, it felt like everything was going to be okay.

Kevin and I sat down on one of the benches. I got a piece of paper, a pencil, and one of my textbooks out of my backpack so we could use it as a hard surface to write on.

Thankfully, after everything that had happened in the library, almost everyone seemed to want to work . . . except Kevin. Although he'd looked happy when he saw the dog, now he looked pretty upset again. I asked him to get out his homework, and he grumpily did what I said without saying a single word.

I needed to figure out a way to cheer him up, stat!

I started by doodling a picture of a dog on the corner of his worksheet. I wasn't particularly good at drawing animals, but I did my best.

A small smile formed on Kevin's lips when he realized what I was doing. "Is that a puppy?" he asked.

"Yeah!" I said. "I can draw other stuff, too, if you want.

What other things do you like?"

"I like the Avengers!"

Aha! Superheroes, I could do for sure.

"Kevin, I want to make you a deal," I said. "We don't have much time left, so we have to focus and work hard if we're going to finish the worksheet by the end of this session. If you promise to work hard and be on your best behavior for the rest of class, I'll draw you as a superhero!"

Kevin's jaw dropped. "Can you really do that?"

"Yeah!" I said. "I'm not the best at drawing animals, but I do draw superhero comics for fun."

"That's so cool! I want a superhero drawing!"

It was like I'd flipped a switch. Thanks to Kevin's burst of motivation, we finished his history homework in almost no time at all.

"Okay, if you could have any superpower, what would you choose?" I asked.

Kevin clenched his fists in excitement. "I'd want to be able to talk to animals, like dogs!"

On a separate piece of paper, I drew Kevin as a superhero surrounded by lots of dogs. They all had their mouths open, like they were having a fun conversation.

"Wow!" Kevin exclaimed when I was done. "This is so good! Thanks, Gigi!"

He was back to being the smiling, happy kid I'd seen playing with my little brother.

"No problem," I said with a grin. "Good job today!"

In the last five minutes of the session, I went around to check in on my friends and their students. They seemed to have been productive for the rest of the sessions too. Today wasn't perfect, but everything had worked out in the end.

When the students were gone, my friends and I exchanged glances. We were *exhausted*.

Zeina raised her eyebrows. "Well, *that* was a day."

"More like a *week*," replied Carolina with a groan. "We definitely need to work out a few kinks here and there."

"Agreed." I nodded. "How about we meet this weekend to talk things over?"

"Sure," replied Carolina. "But my house is off-limits again."

"My house is a no-go, too," Zeina said. "Aya said she needs complete silence for her college essays this weekend. It's just one thing after another with her!"

"I haven't told my parents about the club yet, so I can't host us either," I said. "Should we just meet back here at the library?"

Emma, who'd been quiet this entire time, shrugged and said, "I can host. My parents are busy this weekend, so I'll have the whole house for myself."

"Perfect!" I exclaimed. "Thanks, Emma."

Emma texted Zeina and me her address, and we agreed to meet on Sunday afternoon. After we finished making plans, I left the library, feeling restless.

We still had a *lot* of things to work out!

Eight

I'd hoped my mom would just assume I was going over to Zeina's house again when I left for Emma's the following Sunday, but I had no such luck.

"Where are you off to today?" Mom asked as I headed for the front door.

It was tempting to just lie and tell her I was going over to Zeina's house again, but the Hassans lived way too close for me to pull that off. My parents could randomly stop by at any moment!

"I'm going over to Emma Chen's house to work on a group project," I replied. "She's Carolina's friend and she, Carolina, Zeina, and I are all in the same group for art class."

Of course, Emma wasn't in our art class, but Mom didn't know that. I didn't want to get into the exact details about how I'd gotten to know Emma right now. I was running late already!

"Get home before dinner" was thankfully the only thing Mom said next.

"Okay!"

Since I had to ride my bike to Emma's house, I'd changed out of my usual church dress into a bright red romper. The romper was a little too big for me and was a pain in the butt whenever I had to take it off to go to the bathroom at school, but it was the perfect cute outfit for weekends.

Emma lived in the same part of the neighborhood where Carolina lived. Compared to Zeina's and my houses, their houses were bigger and closer to the community park. I'd passed by Emma's house all the time on my way to Carolina's house or to the park, but this was my first time going into it.

Without having to think much about it, I even knew what Christmas decorations Emma's parents put up every year—a Buc-ee beaver balloon dressed in a Santa suit—and what cars her parents drove—two nice Lexus SUVs—all from just having hung out around this part of the neighborhood.

Emma's house was huge, probably two or three times as big as mine. There were also security cameras all over the place, and even though I knew I'd been invited to the house, I couldn't help but nervously peer up at one as I rang the doorbell.

"Just a moment!"

Footsteps ran up to the door, and Carolina answered with a big smile. Today she had on what she called her Mad Scientist Glasses—round black glasses she wore on days she stayed home. I guess since Emma's house was down the street from hers, she didn't bother wearing contacts like she did anywhere else.

It felt weird to see one of my best friends open the door like she lived in this unfamiliar house. But I knew I shouldn't have been surprised. Like Zeina and I always hung out because we lived next to each other, Emma and Carolina probably did too. Knowing her, Carolina also probably had tons of other friends I didn't even know about.

"Hey!" Carolina said. "We're set up in the kitchen. Follow me!"

We walked through the hall, past a large chandelier that hung down from the high vaulted ceiling. Ornately framed pictures of Emma's parents and Emma as a baby lined the walls as I entered the kitchen.

"Hey," Emma said when we walked in. "Do you want snacks? Help yourself!"

She opened the pantry to reveal rows and rows of snacks. It looked like they had everything from Costco!

I got a bag of Cheetos from the pantry and a can of Sprite from the fridge. My parents never allowed us to have junk food in the house. This was my chance to indulge!

After everyone else had grabbed their snacks, we all sat on the barstools around the kitchen island.

I got the red folder I had for the Ace Squad out of my bag and set it on the counter. I was wondering if anyone would notice that I matched my outfit to the folder when Zeina said, "You look so fancy with that romper and the matching folder!"

I smiled. Zeina was my best friend for a reason.

"Thanks!" I said, before moving on to official business. "Okay, so, we're here to review the first week of the Ace Squad. Put your thumbs up if you think it went well and put them down if you think it was bad."

Carolina put up a thumb, while Zeina held out a sideways thumb and waggled it around a bit. Emma gave a clear thumbs-down.

"Looks like we have mixed responses," I said. "I'd probably give this week a sideways thumb too. Does anyone want to share their thoughts?"

I opened my notebook—which was also red—and waited

for my friends to say something. Carolina got out her tablet to take notes too.

Emma was the first to talk. "It was bad," she said. "We—or at least, I—got kicked out twice! Will we even be allowed to use the library anymore?"

I winced. "Neither was our fault, though . . . like, we weren't the ones yelling and making a scene. So I think it'd be okay as long as there aren't any more fights. It's not like we caused the drama."

"Agreed," Zeina said. "Ms. Kensington is strict, but she seemed to get that neither time was *our* fault. We just have to make sure something like that doesn't happen again."

Carolina tapped her tablet screen with her stylus. "Maybe we should come up with new rules to help us manage the club better. I'll share the file with everyone so we can all access it anytime."

"The first one should be 'no siblings allowed,'" I said almost immediately. "Or, at least, not in the same session. The entire reason Thursday happened is because the twins fought before they even came to the session. It's not fair for us and the other students to get dragged down by family drama that started elsewhere."

"Yeah, my sisters and I wouldn't be able to get anything done if we were in a class together," Zeina said.

"Same with Tommy and me," I replied.

Carolina typed in "no siblings" for rule number one, and I wrote it down in my notebook. I figured it'd be good to have a version of the rules in pen and paper too, just in case.

"Honestly, we should have had this rule sooner!" I exclaimed. "It's not like we don't know what it's like."

"I'm an only child and so is Carolina still . . . kind of," Emma said with a shrug. "So we couldn't have known. But I get it. What else?"

"How about no phones and other toys?" Zeina suggested. "I got so sick of kids playing with slime or waiting for people to quit checking their phones. I don't want to have to be a mean tutor and take things away."

I wrote down, 2.) No phones and toys, and Carolina also added it to her notes.

"That's a good one," I said.

Next Carolina raised her hand. "Can I add one more?" she asked.

"Yeah, of course!"

"How about, 'be nice to the tutors or get out'? Most of the kids this week were nice, but some of them weren't. I told my parents about how one kid was mean to me, and they said we should have this rule so we can kick someone out if they're being mean to us. Kind of like how restaurants have the right to refuse service."

"That's a great idea!" I said. "Wait, you told your parents about the squad?"

"Yeah!" Carolina exclaimed as she typed out the last rule. "How else would they know to give me a ride from the library every day? I could walk home if I absolutely had to, but I live farther away than you and Zeina. It's so much easier to travel by car. Wait, were we supposed to keep it a secret?"

I looked at Zeina, who shook her head.

"I also told my parents. They'd be too suspicious otherwise! They keep track of what assignments I have due in school."

We all looked at Emma, who shrugged.

"I don't think my parents care about what I do after school," she said. "But I did tell them that I was involved in a tutoring club and that I made new friends. They seemed happy about that."

Was I the only member of the Ace Squad who hadn't told her parents about the club? Truthfully, I wasn't sure if I wanted either Mom or Dad to ever find out. They'd probably tell me that I should get rid of the squad, especially if I told them we were raising money to go to the art camp.

As we wrapped up our discussion about the rules, one thing was certain in my head.

I was going to keep the Ace Squad a secret from my parents for as long as I could.

If they found out, then it'd be all over!

Nine

That evening I had some time to work on my portfolio for Starscape. Even though applications weren't due until December, I wanted to submit mine as soon as possible so I could find out if I got in or not. Ms. Williams said we could submit photos of our classwork, but I also wanted to send in pages of Meteor Girl so the committee could see what I did outside school.

Instead of doing a solo page of Meteor Girl, this time, I also drew my other characters. There was Rocketeer, the girl scientist extraordinaire who could build and launch small rockets with the snap of a finger. And there was Poetess, who enchanted people and animals alike with her beautiful words.

I was so focused on trying to come up with a new

character to join the team that I didn't hear Mom until she was right outside my room.

"Gigi? I called you several times, but you didn't answer—"

I whirled around, trying my best to hide what I was working on.

Mom squinted, trying to see past me.

"What is that?" she asked. "Are you working on a project for art class?"

"Yeah!" I blurted out. The half-truth tumbled out faster than anything else.

Mom pursed her lips. "I see. Well, Appa is home, and dinner's ready. Be sure to wash your hands before you come down to eat."

I breathed a sigh of relief. Had I gotten away with things that easily?

By the time I'd finished washing up and sat down at the dinner table, I'd forgotten all about the little moment I had with Mom upstairs. I was sinking my teeth into delicious galbi ribs when Dad said, "Gigi, your mom told me that you were working on some comic book page for art class. Did you finish the rest of your homework already?"

"Yeah," I said. "I finished the worksheet I had for math during study hall, so the only other thing I have left is to study for science. But it's just a quiz tomorrow, not an exam, so I'm not too worried about it. My teacher said it'll be easy."

Dad frowned. I braced myself for what he was about to say. *Here we go.* . . .

"I see," Dad said. "Why don't you study for the quiz before you work some more on the project? Remember, art is just an elective, so make sure to focus on your other, more important classes first."

I bit my lip so I wouldn't argue with Dad and say that art was actually *the* most important class to me. If I started telling him the truth, I just knew that everything—including everything my friends and I were doing to go to Starscape—would spill out of my mouth. I was already a bad liar; I didn't want to test my limits.

"Okay," I answered, trying my best to ignore the sinking feeling in the pit of my stomach. "I'll study for my other classes first."

Throughout the next day, I was in a bad mood. The science quiz was way harder than my teacher said it would be, which was just great because when I got my grade back, my parents were probably going to give me a lecture on how I should have studied more instead of drawing.

I was still so annoyed at what Dad said the previous day. I already didn't like my math and science classes, but whenever

Dad told me to focus on them instead of art, I just ended up hating them even more.

By lunch, I was in such a bad mood that I could barely muster the energy to say hi to my friends when I sat down at our table in the cafeteria.

"Whoa, what's wrong with you, Gigi?" Emma asked. She gave me a lighthearted grin but quickly dropped it when I didn't smile back at her.

"I'm pretty sure I failed the science quiz," I grumbled.

"Oh, the one on reactions?" Carolina asked. "I thought it was pretty easy."

"Well, not all of us are geniuses like you, Carolina!" I snapped before I could stop myself.

Zeina's jaw dropped. So did Emma's. Carolina's eyebrows bunched up.

"Sorry," I mumbled. "I think I just need to eat lunch by myself today."

Mr. Martin sometimes let us hang out in the choir room before class, so I grabbed my lunch and left the cafeteria. No one said a word as I walked away.

Too embarrassed by my outburst, I pretty much ignored my friends during art class, and they ignored me. When it was time for tutoring, though, I tried my best to hide my feelings and pretend everything was okay. I was teaching Carly again today, and I definitely didn't want her to think I was mad at her.

Luckily, when she arrived, Carly had a huge smile on her face. Her happiness was so contagious that I was also grinning by the time she settled into her seat.

"Guess what!" Carly exclaimed. "I got an A on my history test! I get to see the new Marvel movie this weekend, and it's all thanks to you."

"That's amazing!" I replied. "But nah. Sure, I helped, but you're the one who studied hard. You totally deserve the grade."

"Thanks! But yeah, my mom said she wants me to get ahead with this next unit we're learning about, which is why I'm here. Today I'm doing a worksheet on the Declaration of Independence!"

"Great! I can definitely help with that. Let's get started."

I was worried that the Declaration of Independence was going to be too hard for a third grader like Carly, but luckily, once I explained that it was like a kid telling a parent why their rules were unfair, she was able to fill out the who, what, when, where, and why bubbles of the worksheet.

"Tommy said you were a good teacher, and now I see why," Carly said as she left. "Thanks again for helping me get an A on the test, and thanks for today!"

"No problem!" I beamed, and I was still smiling after all the students had left and it was just me and my friends in the study area.

"Looks like someone is in a better mood!" Zeina exclaimed with a sigh of relief. "We were all worried about you."

I turned to see my friends standing around my table. Carolina had her arms crossed in front of her chest, while Zeina and Emma had tense looks on their faces.

My face turned red. "Yeah, sorry, everyone. I was mad at something my dad said last night, and then things just got worse and worse throughout the day. I feel better now, though, but I shouldn't have lashed out like that. That was *not* okay."

Carolina still looked kind of mad at me, but her arms fell to her sides.

"Oh yeah?" Emma asked. "What'd your dad say?"

"Uh . . ." I looked around and accidentally made eye contact with Ms. Kensington, who raised her eyebrows at me.

I gulped. "Actually, let's go talk outside before we get kicked out again."

In the peaceful back area of the library, I told my friends about what had happened with my parents. When I finished, my friends rolled their eyes and groaned.

"Don't listen to him," Zeina said. "Yeah, a lot of people are good at math and science and have good jobs. But there are also people who have good careers as artists. Like your aunt!"

"Her aunt?" Emma asked. "Who's she? Is she a famous artist or something?"

"Basically!" I exclaimed. "She lives in NYC and is super cool. I want to be like her when I grow up."

I pulled up my cousin's Instagram on my phone, and Zeina and Emma gathered around me to see my phone screen. When I went to Yeji-imo's profile, I jumped. Her most recent post was a picture of her and Christiana Moon at brunch!

Love this amazing human being, my sister from another mister. <3 said the caption.

"No. Way," I said.

"Wait, isn't that Christiana Moon?" Zeina asked. "You love her! Are they friends?"

"I guess so!" I squealed.

I had a sudden flash of a scene that was probably too good to ever come true. Yeji-imo, Christiana Moon, and me sitting at brunch in the heart of NYC. Now I *really* had to go to Starscape. I had no other option!

Emma, Zeina, and I oohed and aahed at the rest of Yeji-imo's posts until Carolina said, "Hey, I have to go. My dad's going to arrive soon."

I looked up from my phone to see her walking away.

"I'll see you guys tomorrow!" I told Zeina and Emma. They nodded and waved me off, like they knew I had to go talk to Carolina one-on-one.

I caught up with Carolina, yelling, "Hey, wait up!"

Carolina stiffened and stood still.

"Are we good?" I asked when we were face-to-face. "I'm so sorry again for snapping at you earlier. You didn't deserve it."

I could tell from the frown on Carolina's face that she was still upset. But she sighed and said, "Yeah, I guess. What you said just bothered me a lot, you know? Like, it's not just this one time. I always get the feeling from you and Zeina that I should feel bad for liking and being good at math, science, *and* art. Like, I know y'all don't like math or science, but do you always have to talk about it?"

"Yeah, I get it," I replied. "It's not related to you at all, I promise! And I'm so sorry I made it seem that way today. It's just hard sometimes, having parents that want you to go into fields you're not even good at. My parents treat Tommy so well, all because he's a boy and loves math and science. Meanwhile, they always talk about how they're afraid I'm going to be a starving artist someday or something."

"That must be tough," Carolina replied. "But it's hard for me sometimes, too. Like, my parents always say I'm wasting my time whenever I play video games. They don't realize that there are people out there who make games as a job and that I might want to be one of them one day."

I frowned. Carolina was right. It wasn't fair of me or Zeina to assume Carolina had it easier just because she liked math and science. We all had our own things going on with our parents, whether other people could see them or not.

"Emma is right, you know," I said after a while. "About what she said earlier. I mean, if there's anyone who can be a rocket scientist *and* design video games, it's you!"

Carolina still didn't look completely at ease as she said, "Thanks. I don't know. I'm going to have to go to Starscape and see if I actually like making video games. It's hard to know when you don't even know where to start."

"I have complete faith that you can figure it all out," I said. "We'll all be there with you!"

"Thanks." Carolina grinned. It was a small smile, but it was better than nothing. "And the same goes for you, you know? Like, so what if your parents don't support you in what you want to do? You have us. Forever."

We hugged, and after Carolina's mom picked her up, I rode my bike back home.

Carolina was right. Even if my parents didn't understand me and what I did, it wasn't the end of the world. I had my friends, and I had the work we were doing as the Ace Squad!

Ten

On Thursday after lunch, I was getting my books when someone tapped on my locker door.

I jumped when I saw Paul Kim Wiley standing right behind me. Paul's locker was nowhere near mine, so it was weird to see him in this part of the hallway. Did he come here just to talk to me?

"Hey," he said. He flashed me his pearly white teeth, like he was a movie star.

"Hi!" I gave him a wide smile back before I had a horrifying thought.

Oh no! What if I have something in my teeth? I didn't check!

It was right after lunch, too. Oh well. It was too late now.

I tried my best to be cool as I replied, "Hi."

"So . . . ," Paul started. "My friend Caleb Santiago said your friends started a tutoring club. The Ace Squad, right?"

"Yeah!"

Caleb himself had never mentioned the Ace Squad to me again after the first time I told him about it, so I'd figured he'd forgotten all about it. But I guess I'd been wrong! I made a mental note to thank him during art. Just like I'd hoped, he had ended up telling Paul after all!

"Sorry if this is awkward, but . . . I really need help with math," continued Paul. "I don't get pre-algebra at all, and I need to pass the big test next week because Coach said he's not going to let me play in the next game until I get my class average up. *And* he might bench me for the rest of the season if I keep failing. Do you think you or any of your friends can help me?"

Pre-algebra? Ugh. It definitely wasn't my best subject. But I was doing okay with the current unit. Unlike science, I actually understood what was going on most of the time. I bet I could do it. And it was *Paul*. Asking for our—*my*—help! This could be my chance to be his friend again. And then . . . who knew? Maybe we could even become something more!

I wanted to say yes, right there and then. But I couldn't. I still remembered how Carolina had called Paul cute in the library. And technically, Carolina had first dibs since she was the math/science tutor. I had to ask her if she was okay with me tutoring Paul.

"I'll check with my friends and let you know what they say," I said.

"Great, thanks!" Paul replied. "Let me give you my number."

"Okay," I squeaked. With a shaking hand, I fished out my phone—I was wearing bright orange parachute pants that had deep pockets—and handed it to Paul.

He casually entered his number into my phone, like it was a perfectly normal, everyday thing to do. And maybe it was, for him. Maybe he gave lots of girls his number, and while I felt like my heart was about to burst out of my chest, to him it was just another day of being Paul Kim Wiley.

Don't think like that and calm down! I thought to myself. *It's not even that big of a deal. You guys were friends when you were little!*

Still, I bit back the urge to squeal when he gave me back my phone with his number saved in it.

"See you in choir!" Paul said with a smile.

"Yeah, see you!"

And then he was gone, just like that.

The warning bell rang. I had to run to get to choir on time. But first I needed a moment. I took my books out of my locker and squeezed them tight in my arms.

I had Paul's number!

I was all out of breath by the time I reached the choir room, and even then I was still a full two minutes late to class.

"Hello, Miss Shin," said Mr. Martin as I made my way to my seat. "It's nice to see you've decided to join us."

"Sorry, Mr. Martin!" I replied. "Won't happen again."

Throughout choir, I desperately wanted to sneak a text to my friends to tell them what happened, but Mr. Martin had a strict no phones policy. So I was just going to have to wait until art class to tell my friends. And ask Carolina how she felt about me teaching Paul math.

During class, Paul met my eyes and smiled at me, not once but *twice*.

What is happening? What does that mean?

Several rounds of "Do, Re, Mi" and "My Favorite Things" later, Mr. Martin spread out his arms and made a special announcement.

"Class, I'm so pleased to inform you that I've selected the soloists for this year's fall concert. Our soloists are as follows: for the girls, Melinda Chiu, and for the boys, Donovan Reynolds!"

Everyone cheered. I cheered too, but I was confused. Paul

had done way better than Donovan! Or so I thought, anyway.

I didn't get a chance to talk to Paul before class was over, so I sent him a text on my way to art.

Sorry you didn't get the solo. ☹

Almost immediately, my phone buzzed.

It's ok. I prob wouldn't have had time to practice anyway. Too busy with classes and football.

Before I could chicken out, I texted him back with, I thought you were great. You have a really nice voice.

Thanks! ☺

Not only was Paul replying to my texts right away, but he'd sent me a smiley face! I couldn't stop grinning as I entered the art room. For once, I was the first one at our table, and it seemed like forever until Carolina and Zeina finally arrived.

Before my friends could even sit down in their seats, I blurted out, "Guess who asked me if we could tutor him?"

Carolina raised an eyebrow. "Who?"

Zeina also gave me a curious look.

"Paul Kim Wiley! He needs help with math."

Both my friends' jaws dropped. Zeina looked just plain shocked, while a bright smile erupted on Carolina's face. Uh-oh . . .

"Wow, you *actually* talked to him? *And* he knows our club

exists?" Zeina asked. "That's so cool! I wonder if this means we'll get more students from our grade."

"Well, he found out because I told Caleb about the club, and Caleb told him about us."

At the mention of his name, Caleb turned around from where he was sitting at the table next to us.

"Hey," he said. "Someone say my name?"

"Yeah!" I replied. "Thanks for telling Paul about our club."

"No problem. I'm doing pretty well in math right now, but I know Paul has been struggling for a while. Hope you guys can help him! It'd suck if he was pulled from the team. We really need him to do well this season."

"He's in good hands—"

"I'll try my best!"

Carolina and I had spoken at the same time. I internally groaned.

"Oof, *awkward*," Caleb remarked before he turned back around.

"Wait, what do you mean by *I*?" Carolina asked me. "You don't even teach math."

I sighed. I'd hoped there'd be a better way to bring things up with Carolina.

"I know math is usually your subject," I started. "But Paul is kind of my friend, so I was wondering if you were okay with me teaching him instead?"

Carolina had a weird look on her face. She shared a glance at Zeina, who shrugged.

"Oh," I continued when no one said anything. "Do you guys think it'd be better if Carolina taught him? I mean, I know I'm bad at math, but I'm doing well in class right now. Maybe I can teach him for this unit, and Carolina can take over after that if he still has trouble?"

I let out a weak laugh.

Carolina didn't look happy at all. "If that's what you think is best," she muttered, so quietly that I almost didn't hear what she said.

I gulped. This was exactly the kind of response I was afraid I'd receive from Carolina. *But* she hadn't said no. Excitement burst through me again, swallowing up whatever dread I felt. I wanted to jump up and down and scream.

"Yay, thanks!" I exclaimed. "Let me know if you want to tutor anyone I'd normally teach too. You know, to make things fair."

"Okay," Carolina said.

Her voice sounded funny, but before I could reply, Ms. Williams came into the classroom.

"All right, my wonderful artists!" she said. "Let's get back to work on our self-portraits!"

This week we were working on what Ms. Williams called reflective self-portraits, since they were portraits of ourselves that were supposed to reflect our individual personalities instead of just our physical appearances. I got up and joined the line for the paints and brushes in the back of the room so I could get some for my portrait.

Instead of just drawing me as me, I'd thought it'd be cool if I drew myself as Meteor Girl, since that was the character I drew that was most like myself. Unlike Normal Me, Meteor Girl Me wore a jumpsuit that was the color of the night sky and had on beautiful indigo eye shadow that glittered like the stars above. It was my favorite piece I'd made in school yet, and not just because Ms. Williams had oohed and ahhed when she came over to check my progress.

When Ms. Williams wasn't looking my way, I quickly texted Paul, *Hey, I can tutor you! When is good?*

Paul's reply came right away again. *Awesome! How about Monday afternoon? There's that math test next Friday that I'm nervous about so I want help ASAP.*

I bit my bottom lip. I was pretty sure I already had a kid scheduled for Monday, but it wasn't like we were incredibly busy or anything. Maybe we could switch some things around!

Sounds good. See you then!

I was always excited for the weekend, but for the first

time in a while, I was actually excited for a Monday, too. Next Monday couldn't come fast enough!

Eleven

As soon as I got home from school, I went on our club spreadsheet on my phone. Like I'd guessed, I was currently scheduled to teach Carly on Monday. I really hoped Carly would be able to come at another time.

When we first signed up people for sessions, we'd asked for everyone's numbers and put them all together on one of the sheets. Since Carly didn't have her own phone yet, we had her mom's name and number on the spreadsheet.

Sweat broke out on my forehead as I dialed Mrs. Anderson's number on the phone. Since Carly always got dropped off in front of the library, I never saw her parents. I hoped her mom was nice.

The phone rang. And rang. I thought about hanging up.

But then I thought about how happy Paul had been when I told him we could help. I couldn't give up on him now!

"Hello?" Mrs. Anderson said. Her voice was higher than my mom's but sounded scarier somehow.

I took a quick breath and said, "Hi, Mrs. Anderson, this is Gigi. I'm Carly's tutor. And Tommy's older sister."

"Oh! Hello, Gigi. How are you?" Suddenly, Mrs. Anderson sounded way more friendly than before. "Carly raves about what an awesome tutor you are."

"Really?" I beamed. "That's so great! She's a great student. And so cute, too. I love teaching her! Um, which reminds me. Is it okay if Carly comes a bit later in the day on Monday, at five instead of four?"

"Hm, that should be fine, but let me check our calendars. Are you girls getting busy already? Business must be booming!"

In reality, we weren't *that* busy, since we still had just enough students so that everyone could teach for an hour every day from Monday to Thursday. But Carly's mom didn't have to know that.

"Well, we're just getting started," I said. "But things are starting to pick up!"

"Oh, I can only imagine." There was a brief pause, and then Mrs. Anderson continued. "Five should be fine. I'll just give Carly a snack beforehand. Thanks for the heads-up, Gigi!"

"It's my pleasure!" I exclaimed. "Have a good weekend!"

"You too!"

After we hung up, I grabbed one of my pillows and screamed into it so my parents couldn't hear me. I'd actually done it! I'd made room in my schedule so I could teach Carly *and* Paul.

I had to wait a couple of minutes for my hands to stop shaking. And then I switched back to the club spreadsheet on my phone and added a new time slot column to Monday's schedule. I moved Carly to that column and then put Paul in her original slot.

When I was done, I texted Paul.

Hey! I typed. So, good news. I have you confirmed for 4 PM on Monday at the library.

Paul's reply was instant. Awesome! Thanks a bunch, Gigi. ☺

There it was again! The smiley face. I grinned, thinking about how Paul's real smile brightly lit up his face.

That night after dinner, when I was sure my parents and Tommy had all gone to sleep, I flipped open my sketchbook to the Meteor Girl panel I'd started for my application for Starscape. After what happened with my parents, I'd barely had any time to work on my art. It was just too risky. I definitely didn't want to hear another lecture!

But now, in the quiet of the night, I continued working

on my panel. I wanted to finish tonight so I could turn in my application for Starscape this weekend.

I'd decided to name the fourth character on Meteor Girl's team Fashionista. Fashionista could not only replicate any piece of clothing she saw, but she could also transform into anyone too, even copying exactly how they behaved. Kind of like Mystique from *X-Men*. But with better clothes.

After I was done drawing Fashionista, I added Choir Boy to the page. The panel was starting to look a bit crowded with the new additions, but I managed to squeeze him into a box at the very bottom, calling for help. Meteor Girl and her friends had to act fast to come to his rescue!

I'd just finished the rest of the panel and had started the application for Starscape when my phone buzzed.

I set my pencil down so I could check the screen. It was a text from Carolina.

Hey, Gigi, it read. Did you mess with the schedule?

I opened it, only to see that Carolina had messaged *the entire squad* group chat and not just me.

Before I could respond, Emma joined in.

Wait, since when are we doing two hours? I thought we were going to stick to an hour for now until we got more used to tutoring?

Next was another text from Carolina.

I have no idea. It seems like Gigi is doing whatever she wants now.

My jaw dropped open. *What is happening?* I thought. My head started to spin. Tonight had started off so awesomely. How had things gone so wrong, so fast?

Zeina finally chimed in with, Hey, guys. I'm sure Gigi has a good reason for what she did. Right, Gigi?

I knew I had to reply, but I had no idea what to say. The truth was, I didn't have a good reason for moving things around the schedule, other than that I wanted to make room for Paul. We'd already had an awkward conversation about me tutoring him instead of Carolina. I didn't want another one.

A few minutes passed.

Carolina sent a question mark.

Helloooo? Emma texted. Gigi, are you there?

I let out a shaky breath. I knew I had to say something. Fast.

Hey, guys, sorry! I texted. I was trying to finish up my application for Starscape!

It wasn't a *complete* lie. I *had* been working on my panel before I got all the texts.

My head was still spinning. I didn't know what to say to my friends that could make this situation any better. So I sighed and went with the truth.

Paul said he wanted me to tutor him on Monday, so I asked Carly's mom if Carly could come at 5 instead. She said it was no problem, so I thought it'd be okay. Sorry I didn't tell you guys about it before making the change! I completely forgot.

Emma sent a thinking face emoji, and Carolina sent "..."

Oh well. If Carly's mom said it's all right for her to come later, that's okay, I guess, replied Zeina. I have to go to bed now. Good night, everyone!

Carolina wrote, 'Night, and Emma sent a thumbs-up emoji.

I dropped my phone onto my bedside table with a sigh of relief. That could have almost been a complete disaster.

Hoping everything would just blow over during the weekend, I went back to working on my application for Starscape. Luckily, I had enough money left over from Lunar New Year to pay for the application fee myself. And I already had pictures of the artwork I'd done in class saved on my phone.

I snapped a couple of pictures of the Meteor Girl panel I'd been working on and uploaded them to my computer along with the pictures of the other nine pieces I was submitting. Since the website said we could turn in pictures of our works in progress, I also included a picture of the self-portrait I was working on in class.

The application itself was pretty easy to fill out, with the hardest part being the section where I had to fill out information about my teachers so I could send them recommendation requests.

When I reached the final confirmation page, I hovered my mouse cursor over the submit button and then went back to double-check everything on my application. This was it! There was no going back now.

My heart beat faster as I closed my eyes and thought about Starscape and what it'd be like to open my eyes one morning and just find myself surrounded by skyscrapers and people from all over the world.

Then, finally, I took a deep breath and clicked submit.

Twelve

The rest of the weekend went by slowly, because the only plans I had besides finishing the application were to do my homework and hang out with my family.

I wished I had other plans, because even though I knew it was highly unlikely anyone was reviewing my application over the weekend, I couldn't stop checking my phone every spare moment I had. Even when I couldn't check, like when I had my hands full playing *Overcooked* with Tommy or when I wasn't allowed to have my phone out at dinner, I felt anxious, like I was going to die if I couldn't see if I had gotten any new emails.

I tossed and turned and barely got any sleep on Sunday night. When it was finally Monday morning, I shot up from my bed and checked my phone. Still nothing. My shoulders slumped.

Aside from the fact that I refreshed my inbox every moment I could, Monday went by like any other day. Like I'd hoped, Carolina and Emma didn't mention what happened on Friday, and school was as good as it could be on a Monday. Maybe things weren't as bad as I thought they'd be, after all!

When my friends and I showed up at the library after school, Paul was already there. I got a burst of adrenaline just seeing him sitting at one of the tables. He was better than coffee! Carolina gaped at him, like she couldn't believe her eyes.

"Hey," Paul said, giving us a wave and a smile.

"Hi!" I beamed.

I sat down at the table with Paul, while my friends sat at their own tables. None of the other students were here yet, so I could feel everyone's eyes on us as I asked him, "So, you said you wanted to work on systems of equations, right? How did you do on the quizzes we had this unit?"

"Pretty bad," he replied with a sigh. "I had no idea what was going on or what I was supposed to do. I couldn't even finish all the questions on time. I think I got a forty-something on the first one and fifty-something on the other most recent one."

"Well, at least you're improving?" I replied, trying to be positive.

"Yeah . . . but I literally just picked a random answer for some questions. And I can never finish all the problems on time. I brought the quizzes like you asked so we could go over them."

He got out the packets from his binders.

"Great!" I said. "I mean, not the part about you guessing, but that you came prepared!"

Paul gave me an awkward smile.

I took a deep breath and started flipping through the first quiz. Paul was right; it didn't seem like he knew what he was doing. Entire questions were left blank, or sometimes he'd just circled an answer without doing any work to solve the problems. When I was done going over the entire quiz, I flipped to the first page, where there was a big, scary 45 on the top of the sheet. Instead of focusing on that, though, I tapped my pencil on #3, the first question Paul had gotten wrong.

"Okay, let's start with this one. If you look at this graph over here, you can use it to figure out the solution, which is the point where the two lines meet. Can you show me how you'd normally solve the question so I can see where things go wrong?"

Paul gulped. "I'll try my best."

The only other time I'd seen Paul this nervous was during his choir audition. All the other times, he seemed so confident just walking down the hallways that seeing him like this now was kind of endearing.

"You can do it!" I squeezed his arm in encouragement.

Paul gave me a shy grin that made me all warm and fuzzy inside.

"Thanks," he said.

Halfway into solving the problem, Paul got confused about what he was supposed to do. But with a little nudging from me here and there, he was able to get the right answer!

"Yay, you did it!" I exclaimed. "See, that wasn't so bad, was it?"

"No, not at all," he said. "It's all thanks to you. You're the best teacher I could ask for!"

Since we'd only finished one problem, I knew he was just saying that to be nice. But his words made fireworks go off in my heart anyway.

"Thanks for working hard," I said. "It's nice to see a student so motivated to learn. A lot of the kids who come here don't want to do anything at first."

Paul laughed. "You sound like one of the teachers at school. Are you sure you're not a real teacher? Do you want to become one when you grow up?"

I laughed. "No way. I started tutoring because I always help my little brother, Tommy, with homework. But what I really want to be is an artist! My friends and I are raising money to go to an art camp over the summer."

I stopped myself before I could keep babbling on. Our plans weren't exactly a secret, but this is the first time I'd ever told anyone outside of the squad about our plans. I glanced around to see if anyone was listening to our conversation, but Zeina, Emma, and Carolina were all busy teaching their own students.

"Wow, that's so cool! I hope you guys get to go," Paul said. "You're such a good artist."

My cheeks reddened, but I still nodded. I knew I was good! Ms. Williams and any other art teacher I'd had said as much. It was one of the many reasons I was working so hard to make my dreams come true.

"I am!" I replied. "Which is why I need to go to this art camp—so I can become even better. One of my favorite artists is teaching there this year, and I *have* to meet her. I'm sure it'll help me get into an amazing art school one day and become a professional artist."

"Wow, that's so cool," Paul said again, but more quietly this time. "I love that you already know exactly what you want to be. I'm kind of jealous, actually. I mean, I like playing football, but I have no idea if I even want to try out for the high school team yet. And aside from that . . . I don't know. Singing is also cool, I guess?"

"You're such a good singer!" I exclaimed. "Your audition was amazing. I was so confused when you didn't get the solo."

Paul's cheeks reddened as he said, "It's probably a confidence thing. I know that's something I still have to work on."

"And there's nothing wrong with that!" I checked the time. "Okay, we should probably get back to work. We've only done one problem so far."

Paul laughed. "All right. Here I go. Can you do me a favor?"

I blinked in surprise. "What?"

"If we finish early today, can you show me some more of your art? I'm so curious! I've only seen the ones displayed in the hallway."

I bit my lip. I did have my sketchbook in my backpack, but I'd never shown it to anyone outside my art class before. I hadn't even shown it to Tommy or my parents!

"Okay, sure," I replied. "I'll show you my sketchbook if we have time at the end."

Paul worked hard for the rest of the lesson. By the time we finished working through the questions from the first quiz, we had ten minutes to spare.

Now it was my turn to hold up my end of the bargain. With trembling hands, I got my sketchbook out of my backpack and placed it in front of Paul.

"Wow, you're so talented!" he exclaimed as he flipped through my sketchbook, pausing at some sketches I did of some of my favorite anime characters. "Wait, you watch *Naruto* too?"

"Yeah!"

I was so excited to hear that he also watched my favorite show that I was completely caught off guard when Paul said, "Wait, this drawing. Is this character me?"

I gasped. I'd completely forgotten about Choir Boy!

"Sorry!" I said. "I was just doodling while you sang for your audition. I didn't mean to be creepy, I swear!"

I expected Paul to be mad, but instead he smiled as he inspected my drawing.

"This looks exactly like me. I know I said it already, but wow! You're so good!"

My cheeks burned. "Thanks."

Too soon, it was the end of Paul's session. I was getting stuff ready for Carly when, on his way out, he said, "Hey, so, today was really helpful, and I'd like to come in again on Wednesday since the test is on Friday. Is that okay?"

Behind me, I heard someone cough. I looked around to see Carolina and Emma staring me down. Zeina was busy gathering up her things, but even she paused to glance over at Paul and me.

I bit my lip.

Paul must have noticed my friends staring at us too, because he shot up from his seat and said, "If Wednesday doesn't work, that's totally fine! Just let me know."

Just then Carly walked into the study area and sat at my table.

"Hi!" she said. "Wow, it feels so weird to come this late!"

So much was happening all at the same time!

"Um, yeah, sorry," I quickly replied to Paul. "I'll look at the schedule and text you later!"

"Sounds good! See you at school."

"See you!"

Paul walked away, and I turned back to my friends. Carolina and Emma had their eyebrows raised, and even Zeina looked confused.

I knew I had to talk to my friends, but I couldn't *right now*. Not when Carly was waiting for me to begin our session.

"I'll talk to you guys tomorrow?" I said. "Sorry!"

"Sure," said Zeina as she walked past me. "See you, Gigi!"

"Yeah, see you," Carolina said as she left. But instead of

sounding friendly like Zeina, Carolina's voice was low, like it was when she was annoyed.

Emma just shrugged and waved as she walked by.

I waved back and then turned to Carly.

"Sorry about all that," I said. "Let's begin."

Thirteen

The next morning I checked my phone and again saw no new emails. Trying to shove away thoughts about Starscape so I could focus on the day ahead, I walked into the school. Carolina was at her locker, so as I passed by, I said, "Hi, Carolina!"

She didn't respond. The hallway *was* noisy, though, so she probably hadn't heard me.

I doubled back.

"Hey!" I said, more loudly this time.

She still didn't respond. Maybe she was too busy looking for something in her locker?

I tapped her shoulder. She *had* to notice me now!

But Carolina still didn't acknowledge me. Instead, she just

slammed her locker shut and pushed past me without even glancing at me.

My jaw dropped. *Is she mad at me?*

I thought back to what happened yesterday. Did me teaching Paul bother Carolina *that* much? Or maybe there was something else that made her upset. I thought that it would be fine once we talked it all out together later today at lunch, but now I wasn't so sure.

"Carolina!" I called out. "What's going on?"

She kept walking away from me without saying a single word.

My friends and I all sat at the same table at lunch, so there was no way Carolina could ignore me then. I gritted my teeth and braced myself for the day ahead, hoping everything would work out in the end.

The lines were always super long at the beginning of lunch, so I stopped by our table before I got food. Zeina was already there with the lunch she had brought from home, but no one else was there yet.

Zeina always liked to eat fast so she could have plenty of time to read for the rest of lunch.

"Hey!" she said between bites of her food.

"Hi," I said. "Did you notice that Carolina is acting weird

lately? She totally ignored me this morning!"

Zeina cocked her head. She swallowed her mouthful of food and asked, "Really? She seemed fine today, or she did to me at least. We talked about *Final Fantasy!*"

I furrowed my brows. So it was just as I'd thought. Carolina was mad at me, most likely because of what had happened yesterday at the library.

I wanted to ask Zeina for her opinion on everything that was going on, but it was probably better to talk about everything once everyone was at the table.

So I said, "Okay, thanks," and went to stand in line for food. I was almost at the start of the line when I spotted Emma and Carolina coming out of the lunch line. They were too far away for me to call out and say hi but close enough that I could see them chatting and laughing like usual.

Maybe I don't have to say anything after all! I thought. *Everything seems normal with the two of them.*

But then, as I watched, instead of going over to our usual table, Emma and Carolina headed the opposite way. They weren't even planning on sitting with us for lunch today!

When it was my turn to grab food, I got a hamburger, some fries, and chocolate milk from the lunch line and returned to our table. Zeina had finished eating and was now nose-deep in a fantasy book about training dragons instead.

"Hey, do you know why Carolina and Emma aren't sitting with us today?" I asked. "I saw them leave the line and go all the way over to the other side of the cafeteria!"

"That's strange!" Zeina said without looking up from her book. "Maybe they decided to eat with another friend today? Carolina and Emma have other friends that we're not close with, right?"

"Maybe."

I could wait until art class to confront Carolina, but today was the last day to work on our self-portraits, so everyone was bound to be stressed out and on edge. The last thing I wanted to do was cause a commotion when everyone needed the time to work.

"I'll be right back," I told Zeina before getting up from our table.

Zeina glanced up from her book. I must have looked upset because her eyebrows bunched up together with worry. "Do you need backup? I saw how tense things got at the library. And the group chat!"

"Um . . . yeah, that's probably a good idea. Thanks!"

Zeina solemnly nodded as she shut her book. "Okay! Let's go."

We gathered up our things and went looking for Carolina and Emma on the other side of the cafeteria. It took us a while, but we finally spotted them near the back wall with a bunch of kids I didn't know.

When we approached them, Emma gave me a nervous look, while Carolina glared up at me. Okay, yeah. Carolina was *definitely* mad at me.

"Hey," I said. "Is there something wrong? You seem upset with me."

Carolina gave Emma a meaningful look before glancing away.

Emma sighed and told me, "She's mad because you tutored Paul when she's supposed to be the one who teaches math."

I looked at Carolina. "But you told me you were okay with it!"

I was afraid Carolina would make Emma talk for her again when Carolina glared at me herself and replied, "Not really! Just because I said 'if that's what you think is best' doesn't mean I was okay with it. Besides, that isn't even the main problem here."

I stood there for a minute, trying to make sense of what Carolina was saying.

"Okay, then what is? Is this about me changing up the schedule? Honestly, I don't understand why that was such a big deal, either. I was responsible and made sure Carly and her mom were okay with the change. Why can't we all just teach whoever we want, when we want? It doesn't matter as long as we all get students, right?"

When I stopped talking, all three of my friends were completely quiet. Carolina was full-on glaring at me now, while Emma looked annoyed. Even Zeina bit her lip and stared at the ground.

"Right?" I repeated myself, my voice coming out shaky and unsure.

No one said anything for the longest time. But then Zeina finally said, "Gigi, I'm sorry to say this, but sometimes it feels like you just expect us to go along with everything you want to do. Like, even with this whole Ace Squad thing . . . like, sure, we all want to go to Starscape, but you didn't even give any of us a chance to come up with other ideas before you charged full steam ahead with this club."

Carolina took a deep breath and said slowly, "Even the name 'Ace Squad.' I didn't like it, and you just went with it."

"Zeina said she liked it, so I was just going with the majority . . . ," I started to reply, but then I stopped. "I guess I should have tried to find a name all of us liked because there was only the three of us at the time. And asked if you guys had any other ideas besides the club."

"Look, I wasn't there for all that drama," Emma cut in. "But from what I saw, it kind of felt like an unfair dictatorship. You told us all what subjects we should teach and when. But the moment some cute boy came along and the rules we established no longer worked for you, you just decided to change them!"

"And you changed the schedule without talking to any of us," added Carolina. "Sure, I like Paul too, so I was annoyed about that. But what wasn't okay was that you were just doing whatever you wanted. The Ace Squad may have been your idea, but it's still *our* club!"

Realization crashed down on me like one final big wave. I felt cold from head to toe as I looked at all my friends one by one. The entire reason I even came up with the Ace Squad in the first place was because I wanted to go to Starscape with my friends. But I'd been so selfish, thinking only about what I wanted instead of seeing how it was affecting everyone else until it was almost too late! Or at least I hoped it was *almost* and not *really* too late.

"Guys," I said. "I am so, so sorry. I was so excited about us raising money for Starscape and was so focused on everything that's been going on back home and with Paul that I've been a horrible friend. Can you guys forgive me? I promise to do better from now on."

Carolina exchanged glances with Emma and then with Zeina. Then all three of my friends turned to look at me. No one said anything for a solid minute.

"No," Emma suddenly said matter-of-factly. "We can't forgive you. In fact, we're banning you from the Ace Squad right now. And getting a guillotine!"

No one said anything for a few seconds. And then everyone burst out giggling.

"A guillotine?" Zeina cried out, choking with laughter. "That's so extreme."

Emma shrugged, giving us all a mischievous grin. "It's literally one of the only things I remember from social studies last year. Off with their heads!"

Emma made a line across her neck with her pointer finger, making us laugh even more.

When we all finally calmed down, Zeina said, "Okay, okay, I forgive you, Gigi. But of course, Carolina and Emma might feel differently."

We both looked at our other two friends. Emma looked like she was resisting the temptation to crack another silly joke, while Carolina seemed a lot less tense than before.

"I'm all right as long as Carolina is okay," Emma finally said. "Honestly, I was just here for the drama." After a playful nudge from Carolina, she added, "And to support Carolina, of course! Duh."

"And you, Carolina?" I asked, turning to my other best

friend. I still felt bad for how I'd treated her over the past couple of weeks. I hoped she could forgive me for everything that happened.

"I think there are a lot of things about the club that we still need to work on and talk about," she said slowly. "But I forgive you, Gigi. Let's all meet up again sometime this weekend. My parents are going to be busy setting up the nursery with my grandparents on Saturday, so I can host everyone at my place this time."

"Sounds good," I agreed, holding out a French fry from my lunch tray. "French fry?"

Carolina held out a Tater Tot for me. "Sure. Tater Tot?"

We exchanged snacks with a smile, and the rest of our friends cheered.

Now I knew we were *really* good.

fourteen

friday was our big pre-algebra test. I didn't have it until seventh period, but I knew Paul had it in first. Along with the two sessions he had with me, he'd been working so hard all week to study for it. I hoped he would do well!

When the day went on and I hadn't heard anything from Paul, I started to worry. Carolina was the better math teacher. Maybe I should have let her teach him after all!

But when I went to drop my books off before lunch, I saw Paul standing in front of my locker. He was smiling. I breathed a sigh of relief.

"Hey," he said. "So obviously I haven't gotten the test back yet, but I think it went well! Or at least as well as it could have. I was able to finish all the questions. That's a first for me!"

"That's so good to hear. I'm sure you did a lot better then!"

"I definitely hope so. We'll get our grades back next week, so we'll know how I did then."

"I'm crossing my fingers and toes for you!"

"Thanks." A heartbeat later, Paul added, "By the way, if I did do bad, or I guess even if I did well but have some mistakes I want to go over, can I come in for tutoring again with you? You were a big help this week, so I'd love to have some more sessions with you."

I beamed. "Yeah, of course!" I answered before I could stop myself. I winced as I remembered what my friends and I had talked about. "Wait, actually, I'm going to have to check with my friends to see if they're okay with me teaching you again. I'm usually the social studies teacher, not the math teacher. So it might be better if you went with Carolina this time."

"Well, okay," Paul replied with a frown. "I'm sure Carolina is a good teacher and all, but I'd rather have you if it's possible. I'm more comfortable with you."

A shy smile spread across his lips as he said the last part, making me grin as well.

"No promises," I said. "But I'll do my best and let you know what they say."

"Sounds good. Thanks, Gigi."

That night I dreamed about what my future might look like with Paul, like us going to the seventh-grade dance in the spring and going on cute dates to the mall. And after I woke up, I spent Saturday sketching out the different cute outfits I'd wear to cheer for him at football games.

But when Sunday came along, I knew it was time to get down to business.

After lunch the four of us all met up at Carolina's house. I didn't notice it before since I hadn't gone to Emma's house yet, but now I saw that Carolina's house was a mix of the three of our houses. Size-wise, it was about halfway between Emma's and mine, but a lot of interior things, like the paint on the walls and the stairwell, had features of both houses.

Before Carolina's mom got pregnant with her baby sibling, both Zeina and I were so jealous of Carolina because she was an only child. Carolina had *two* rooms all for herself, a bedroom covered in sky blue wallpaper with lots of different kinds of airplanes and her own personal study, which she used as a laboratory. But now, since the study was being made into the baby's nursery, Carolina's bedroom was crammed with her bookshelves, bed, test tubes, and desk all in one room.

"Sorry for the mess," Carolina said as we walked in. "I'm going to get my dad's old office since he doesn't work from home anymore, but he won't have time to set it up for me until after my parents finish the nursery. So I have to live like this for now."

"So exciting!" Zeina clapped her hands. "Are you looking

forward to becoming an older sister?"

Carolina shrugged. "Most of the time, yeah! But on days like this, no." She gestured at the crowded room around us. "I miss being an only child."

"This is fine!" Emma said, plopping down on Carolina's Planet Earth rug. She patted the floor beside her. "There's plenty of room for all of us on this chunk of rock."

Grinning, Carolina, Zeina, and I joined Emma on the circular rug. It was a little cramped, but it was still cozy and nice. I thought about the days in kindergarten when we would all sit in a circle on the floor. Zeina was my only friend then, but now I also had Emma and Carolina sitting with me. It was a weird but definitely nice feeling.

"So," started Carolina. "I think we should make an official club amendment to the rules."

She got out her tablet and opened the shared document, where she'd written down our original rules. I got out my notebook as well.

"Kind of like how the Founding Fathers had to make amendments to the Constitution?" I asked. It's what Carly and I had worked on in our last session together, so the Constitution was still fresh on my mind.

"What sort of amendment do you think we need?" Zeina asked.

"Well, first of all, I think we should make an amendment that says that all tutors can teach whatever they feel comfortable teaching as long as they get the head tutor's permission and everyone agrees that is what's best for the student," Carolina replied. "I feel like this would have saved a lot of awkwardness between Gigi and me."

"I totally agree," I replied, grateful that Carolina brought everything up first. "So, like, if any of you wants to teach history, you can ask me. And after we all talk about it and agree that that's best, you can teach it instead of me. And same with Carolina and math or science, Zeina with English, and so on."

Emma exchanged glances with Carolina before saying, "We should also add that the head tutor is allowed to say no, for whatever reason."

I bit my lip. I could tell she was saying this because of what happened between Carolina and me. "That's a good idea," I replied.

Carolina typed out the amendment below our original rules.

"Okay, is there anything else we should add to the rules?" Zeina asked.

"If you don't follow the rules," Emma started to say, "you'll be beheaded by guillot—oof!"

Carolina elbowed her, making everyone—including Emma herself—laugh.

"Okay, other than the guillotine," Zeina continued with a smile. "What else is there? Oh, I know. Changes to the schedule! There was some drama about that, too, right?"

I winced. I'd completely forgotten about that part, probably because it'd been so embarrassing.

"The second amendment should be that any change made to the schedule shouldn't be done without talking about it with everyone," I said. "I definitely messed up big-time with that."

Since we were talking about it anyway, I turned to Carolina and added, "By the way, again, I am so sorry for just putting Paul on my schedule without asking you first. If you want, we can move him to your schedule for next week! He said he wants help reviewing the questions he got wrong after we get the tests back."

Carolina looked thoughtful, and I held my breath. A part of me couldn't help but hope that she would let me keep teaching Paul.

Finally, Carolina shook her head. "No, it's okay. It's probably not good to switch tutors on him now. Maybe we can switch him over to me for the next unit. For now, though, I'm okay with leaving things the way they are. Maybe we can just see what happens and see who he gets along with the most?"

"Sure! That works. Thanks, Carolina."

We hugged it out, and our friends cheered.

Emma whooped.

"Thank God," she said. "To be honest, before we talked about everything last week, I thought the Ace Squad was done for! I'd just gotten the hang of tutoring, too."

Zeina nodded. "Same here. It's challenging, but it's fun, too!"

"The money definitely helps," Carolina added, making us all laugh. "When things get bad during a session, I remind myself that I'm getting closer and closer to being able to go to Starscape, and that helps a *lot*."

My friends and I all laughed.

"Oh, by the way," I said. "I submitted my application! Did any of y'all finish yours too?"

Zeina raised her hand. "I did! Haven't heard back, though."

"Me neither," I replied. "How about the rest of you?"

Carolina shook her head. "I'm trying to finish up a couple of more character designs before I submit them for my application."

Emma looked nervously around at all of us. "Honestly, I probably won't end up submitting until the very last minute. Since I'm not in art class like the rest of you, I still have a lot of designs to finish first."

"That's okay," I said. "You still have the rest of this month and November!"

"Let us know if you need help with anything," Carolina told Emma. "It must be tough trying to catch up with everyone. Ms. Williams is pretty chill with us taking supplies from art class as long as we bring them back the next day, so we can borrow some for you, too."

"Yeah, just let us know!" Zeina said.

Emma rounded all of us up for a group hug. "Thanks, guys. You're the best."

"No problem," I said. "We have your back!"

"Right now, quite literally," Emma joked.

"You bet!" I replied.

Everyone laughed as we pulled apart.

Since we were only in our first few weeks of tutoring, we were still a long way from our goal of having enough money saved for Starscape. But I was feeling more confident than ever that my friends and I could achieve what we all set out to do.

fifteen

I didn't get much of a chance to relax after making peace with my friends because later that afternoon my phone buzzed as I was coming home from the library.

STARSCAPE YOUNG ARTISTS' PROGRAM APPLICATION DECISION, the email notification said. *Greetings, thank you for applying to the Starscape Young Artists' Program....*

That was it. That was all I could see of the email from just the notification.

As much as I wanted to find out whether I got in, I didn't want to find out in the middle of the street. What if I didn't get in and had a breakdown in public? The neighbors would call my parents for sure.

So instead of tapping on the notification, I sped up and ran home. I was wearing my pink floral overalls today, so I was able to keep up a good pace. When my house was finally in sight, I tapped the notification and was about to read the email when . . .

I saw that both my parents' cars were in the driveway. Dad wasn't usually home this early, so something must be wrong.

My hand hadn't even touched the doorknob when the front door swung open. Mom and Dad both stood in the doorway, looking *really* mad. At me.

I shoved my phone into the front pocket of my overalls and glanced at Zeina's house. Maybe it wasn't too late for me to make a run for it now. I could hide out there until my parents calmed down.

"Don't even think about it," Dad said when he saw where I was looking. "Your umma and I have serious things to talk to you about."

I sighed. It was worth a shot.

"Gigi, did you check your grades recently?" Mom asked, her voice tight with concern. "Why didn't you tell us that you failed your most recent science quiz? And not just Asian fail, but completely!"

My jaw dropped. The science quiz! I'd been so caught up with everything that'd happened in the last couple of weeks that I'd completely forgotten about it. Mr. Roberts hadn't passed our quizzes back in school yet, but he must have entered the grades today.

Mom made a *tsk-tsk* sound while Dad shook his head in disapproval.

"See, I told you we should have stopped her from running the tutoring business," he said to Mom in Korean. "She's been so busy with it that it's affecting her ability to do everything else!"

I didn't think my jaw could open even more, but it did. If a bug came flying into my mouth at this very second, I wouldn't have been surprised.

"You know about the tutoring business?" I finally managed to cry out.

"Of course!" Mom said. "We're not stupid. The other day we were talking to Mr. Hassan while he was taking out the trash and he mentioned the club. When we told him we had no idea at all about this 'Ace Squad,' he looked shocked. We were so embarrassed!"

"But wait," I replied, glancing back and forth between Mom and Dad. "I don't get it. If you knew about it, why didn't you say anything?"

"Because," Dad said. "Even though we didn't necessarily like the idea, we thought it wasn't doing any harm. But now . . ." He harumphed and then continued in English. "How do you expect to properly teach others if you're failing yourself?"

"Your father and I are so disappointed in you," Mom said, also in English. "What made you think this was okay? And why did you even start this whole tutoring thing in the first place?"

I wanted to argue back to my parents, tell them it was just one quiz grade and it wasn't like I was failing the entire class. I wanted to tell them that what they were saying wasn't even relevant because it wasn't like I was teaching science. I was teaching social studies! But I bit my lip. I knew my parents too well. If I tried defending myself, it would just make everything worse.

But still, if there was anything I learned from what happened this past week, it was that honesty was the best policy. So I took a deep breath. My voice was shaking, but I responded as slowly and as calmly as I could.

"I'm sorry about the science quiz. I should have paid more attention and studied harder. And I will! I promise. The good news is, it's just a quiz, so if I do well on the test, that should more than make up for it. I'll study hard and even ask Carolina for help if I have to. I'm confident that I won't fail the class."

Mom pursed her lips. Dad raised his eyebrows, looking semi-convinced.

"And," I continued, still trying my best to maintain my slow and calm pace. "The only reason I started this business with my friends was because you and Mom didn't take me seriously when I said I wanted to go to art camp. I feel like you're always willing to support Tommy in what he wants to do but not me. It's not fair. But I know we can't afford the camp, even if you guys wanted to help, so I just wanted to pay for myself without being a burden to you and Mom."

My parents blinked. They looked at each other for a long moment.

And then Mom said in Korean, "Gigi, we're sorry if we made it seem like we didn't care about your future or what you want to do. Of course we do. We just want to make sure you choose something that would be more worth the money and time, that's all."

"Like science or math," Dad added.

I sighed. "But I'm so bad at science and math. The quiz is proof of that. Carolina was telling me that the quiz was so easy for her. That just shows how bad I am in comparison."

I was afraid my parents would keep on telling me I should just study harder, but they didn't. Mom shook her head, while Dad sighed.

"Okay. I guess that can't be helped, and we can figure out a solution some other time. But as for everything you said about the camp and Tommy . . ." Dad sighed. "He's over at Lionel's place so we can talk about it now, but don't tell him this when he gets back home. The truth is, we probably won't be able to send him to robotics camp. Of course, things may change between now and next summer, but business has been slow, and there's no guarantee they'll get better by spring, when summer camp applications are due. Luckily, Tommy is still very young, so if he can't go this year, we can always send him next time."

"Oh," I replied. It made me sad to hear that Tommy wouldn't be able to go to summer camp, either. It sucked sometimes to not be able to afford things that a lot of other kids at my school took for granted.

Regardless of whether or not we could afford camp, though, Mom and Dad *did* pretty much say that art was a waste of time.

So I continued. "It's okay if you can't afford to send us to camp. That's why I started our tutoring club! But art *is* something that is going to be worth my time. Sure, I still have to figure out how to get into art school and how to make it my job after that, but I've never been more serious about anything!"

I got out my phone. Gritting my teeth, I unlocked it. It'd be so embarrassing if, after all this, I'd gotten rejected from Starscape.

But instead of a just being short apology message, the

email continued on to say . . . *We are pleased to inform you that you have been selected as one of the artists in the seventh-grade program. Congratulations!*

"I got in!" I yelled. "Umma, Appa, I got in!"

Mom and Dad jumped at my reaction and slowly took the phone from me. I watched my parents as they read the email. I wanted to give them both a hug, but I knew the timing wasn't right. At least, not yet. Dad's eyebrows shot up, like they did when he was impressed.

"It says here that they select only a few students out of tens of thousands from all over the world every year," he said. "This sounds really prestigious!"

"It is!" I said. "Ms. Williams said it'll look amazing on college applications."

Mom pursed her lips again. She didn't look as convinced as Dad did, so I kept my gaze on her as I said, "Before you make any decisions, let me show you something."

Even Paul, an almost stranger when I first taught him, was impressed by my sketchbook. Surely this meant that my parents would be impressed by my sketchbook too!

I got out my sketchbook from my backpack. I'd hidden it from them for all this time because I was afraid of what they would say about it. But maybe now was the time to show them what I've been working on. They couldn't say no after seeing all my hard work, right?

I held out my sketchbook to my parents, and they carefully took it from me. As they slowly flipped through the pages, their eyes went wide. I couldn't tell if they liked what they saw or not.

"I want to be an artist," I went on, squeezing my eyes shut so I wouldn't have to keep looking at their reactions. "And I want to go to this camp. If you guys end up being able to afford it, I *want* you to send Tommy to robotics club, since he's too little to raise money on his own like I can. But please let me continue this club so I can go to art camp. I promise to study hard and keep my grades up."

When I finally opened my eyes, my jaw dropped wide open *again*.

Mom was crying! And so was Dad!

My parents almost never cried, and the only times I'd seen them do so were at funerals. I didn't know what to say, so I stared down at my feet and waited for them to speak.

"This is amazing," Mom finally said in Korean. "You really are talented. You're possibly even better than Yeji-imo was at your age."

I gasped. Yeji-imo was who I always looked up to, who I wanted to be when I grew up. And Mom thought I was better than her? I couldn't even imagine what that meant.

"Yes, you're clearly very talented," Dad agreed, wiping the tears from his eyes. "And I'm sorry your umma and I didn't recognize it sooner. But the tutoring club . . . I don't know, Gigi. I still think it is a bad idea for you and your friends to continue tutoring. You're all kids! What if things go wrong? It's only been a few weeks and it's already affecting your grades. And you or your friends can easily make a mistake. What if your students still get bad grades after your help, and people get mad? Things would get too complicated. Maybe you should find a different way to raise money for the camp."

I shook my head. "My grades, I can fix. I promise. And as for the club, we're doing a good thing. I can prove it! Yeah, the club might still need a few adjustments here and there, but we've only been doing this for a month, and people are already telling us what a big help we've been."

My parents gave me a confused look.

"You can prove it?" Dad asked. "How?"

Dad's gaze was so focused on mine that it felt like he could see through my insides. It was so tempting to just give in to the pressure and come up with a random idea on the spot. But after everything that happened with my friends and me, I knew that wasn't the right thing to do. The club wasn't just mine. It also belonged to my friends. And together, we could come up with an awesome idea to save it.

"I need to talk to my friends first," I said. "But I'll tell you and Mom as soon as we decide what to do. Please give us some time?"

Mom and Dad looked at each other. Dad still seemed unsure, but Mom reluctantly nodded.

"Okay," she said. "But this doesn't mean we're saying yes to keeping the club. We might still say no after everything."

"That's fine," I replied. "Just give us a chance! You won't regret it, I promise."

"Okay." Mom squeezed my hand. "We'll see."

"For now, though," Dad said. "You and your friends should stop teaching. Your mom and I don't think it's a good idea until all the parents are okay with it. And you need to study for the science test."

I clenched my fists. I knew for a fact that all my friends' parents were okay with the Ace Squad. It was literally just my parents. But I knew that if I pushed too hard now, my parents might never be okay with the club.

"Okay, that's fine," I said again. "I can't control what my friends do but I'll stop tutoring for now until I can prove to you and Mom that we're doing a good thing. And I'll go study science *right now*."

"Good," Mom replied. "Thank you, Ji-Young."

I went to my room. After I'd reviewed the chapter in my

science textbook about reactions, I sent out a group text to my friends.

Can we do a video chat meeting tonight?? There's a bit of an emergency!

Zeina responded first. OMG is everything ok? Are you ok?

Yeah! Dw it's not that kind of emergency. More like club business emergency.

Everyone else responded, and we all agreed to have a virtual meeting in two hours. I crossed my fingers. I hoped my friends and I could find a way out of this mess!

Sixteen

At eight p.m. my friends and I all joined the virtual meeting. Since I saw them in person at school every day, it was weird to see the three of them on my phone screen now. Zeina was in her room, surrounded by her books and plants as always. Carolina had on her Mad Scientist Glasses, and there was a pencil tucked behind her ear. And Emma was in what I assumed was her room, which was decorated like Barbie's pink paradise bedroom. Zeina and I giggled when we saw Emma's space because it was the complete opposite of her usual all-black aesthetic.

"So, what's up?" Carolina asked when we were all settled in.

"Well . . . ," I said, drawing out the word for several seconds.

"I have good news and I have bad news."

"Bad news first!" Emma blurted out before anyone else could say anything.

Carolina nodded. "Yup. Bad first so the good softens the blow."

I let out a quick breath.

"Okay, well. My parents found out about the Ace Squad," I said. "And they want us to quit. Or, I guess, they want *me* to quit, since they can't really say what *you guys* can or can't do."

Zeina slapped her forehead. "Was it my parents? I know I should have told them not to say anything!"

I shook my head. "It's not your fault, Zeina. My parents were bound to find out eventually, and apparently they've actually known the truth for a while now. They just didn't have a problem with it until I failed the last science quiz. If it's anyone's fault, it's mine."

"Oh shoot!" Carolina said. "Gigi, feel free to ask me for help. I'll tutor you too if I have to. Maybe I can give you a fifty percent fellow squad member discount."

I grinned at the thought. "I honestly think I just have to study more. But if I do need help, I'll for sure come to you. But yeah, I wish my parents were more open-minded like y'all's parents."

My friends all looked worried.

"Wait," Emma said after a while. "What was the good news?"

"Well," I replied, my voice coming out quiet and shaky. "I got into Starscape! Although, with everything that happened with my parents, I don't know if I could even go anymore."

"We have to figure something out!" Emma exclaimed. "Congrats, by the way. I'm still working on my application."

"Yeah, congratulations, Gigi!" Zeina exclaimed. "I actually found out that I got in today, too . . . but it didn't seem like the right time to say anything."

"What?" I asked. "Of course it's the right time! Why wouldn't it be?"

Zeina shrugged. "I'd feel bad if I could go but you couldn't."

I shook my head. "No, I'm so glad you got in. Worst case scenario if I end up not being able to go, I'd be so happy to hear that you're there!"

"It'd be so tragically funny if Zeina ends up being the only one from the Ace Squad to make it to camp . . . ," Emma said. "Wait, how about you, Carolina? Have you turned in your application?"

"I'm actually *just* about done with everything," replied Carolina. "I was planning on submitting things by this weekend!"

Emma clapped her hands to her cheeks. "Wait, what if *I* end up being the only person here who doesn't make it? I'm not even close to being done!"

"You still have plenty of time," I reassured Emma. "Just make sure to finish by December!"

"Wait, so . . . ," Zeina said to me. "Do your parents want you to quit, like, right now?" asked Zeina. "I can ask my parents to talk to them!"

Carolina nodded. "I can ask my parents too!"

"I don't know if my parents will be any help because they don't know them yet," Emma added. "But I can ask as well."

I shook my head. "That might help, but I think what will really convince them even more is if—along with me raising my grade—we show them how much the Ace Squad has helped the students. They said they'd give me a chance to prove that we're doing a good thing."

"Hmmm." Carolina scrunched up her face like she did whenever she was trying to solve a difficult problem.

I thought hard too, trying to think of a way to convince my parents to let us continue the business. And that's when I got a possibly terrible but also possibly ingenious idea.

"What if we have a big party?" I asked. "To celebrate the first month of our club. We can invite a bunch of our existing students and their parents so they can meet with my parents.

And we can invite y'all's parents as well, so they can all talk together. It'd be like knocking down two birds with one stone!"

Carolina opened her mouth wide. "That's an amazing idea! We could even knock down *three* birds, because I bet if we said we're going to have a party, it'll attract the attention of more people from school. I don't know about you guys, but only teaching little kids is getting exhausting."

"What kind of party should we throw?" Zeina asked. "I've never been invited to a party before, or at least, not the kind of party that the cool kids have. And I'm not sure that kind of party would be a good idea in these circumstances, either."

Emma laughed. "It'd be so funny if we did, though. Can you imagine our parents' faces?"

Despite the seriousness of the situation, I couldn't help but grin at the thought. My other friends all smiled too. We could always rely on Emma to make us laugh with her silly jokes.

"I know," Carolina said. "How about we host a fun arts and crafts night, where everyone can hang out while making art and eating snacks? Since we're raising money to go to art camp and all."

My other friends and I snapped to attention, oohing and aahing at the idea.

"Sounds fun!" Emma exclaimed. "I can host at my house. My parents keep bugging me to have people over anyway. They always think, as an only child, I need more socializing. Apparently just having Carolina over all the time isn't enough."

"Ouch, haha," replied Carolina. "I get it, though. But also, that's so funny! You're like the only one of us who's *been* to actual parties!"

Emma mischievously shrugged and put a finger to her lips. "Well, yeah, but they don't know that."

We all laughed again. When everyone settled down, I said, "Okay, so, like Carolina said, let's invite all the current students and their parents and encourage them to invite their friends too. That way, word will spread without us having to do much!"

Everyone nodded in agreement. My heart beat faster in excitement. I was glad I had friends who could help me figure out an amazing solution. And I was so looking forward to asking Paul to come to the party! Hopefully, as one of the most popular kids in our school, he'd bring a lot of people who could also become our students.

"Thanks so much, y'all," I said before we hung up. "I'm so glad and grateful to have all of you as my friends. If there's one thing I'm learning from all this, it's that brainstorming as a group is *way* better than trying to figure everything out yourself."

Carolina smiled. "Duh, it's literally four brains versus just one!"

We all laughed one last time before we ended the call.

Before I went to sleep later that night, I logged on to Instagram. From finding out that I got into Starscape to brainstorming with my friends about how to convince my parents, so much happened in one day. Just thinking about everything was enough to make my heart beat faster.

I went on to Aunt Yeji's Instagram and clicked the Direct Message button. To my surprise, I saw that Min-seo had already sent lots of messages to Yeji-imo. They had full-on conversations about everything from the weather in NYC to the best brunch places in the city!

Then again, I shouldn't have been surprised. Yeji was Min-seo's aunt too, not just mine.

Before I could chicken out, I typed with shaking hands, *Hi, Yeji-imo! This is Gigi. I'm using Min-seo's Instagram to contact you since I don't have my own Instagram yet. I don't know if you know what it is, but I got into the Starscape Young Artists' Program. It's going to be at NYU this year! I don't know if I can go yet, but if I do end up being able to go, I'd love to see you in NYC while I'm there!*

I clicked send and spent the next ten minutes refreshing

messages. No response. Not even the "seen" label. It *was* pretty late in NYC. Maybe she just didn't check social media at night.

Since I didn't want Min-seo to see my aunt's response before I did, I muted the conversation and exited the app.

My next unit test for science was on Friday, so my friends and I planned the party to be after school the following afternoon. It sucked to just come straight home from school every day to study one of my least favorite subjects, but I grit my teeth and buried my head in my books.

During my breaks, I checked Instagram to see if Yeji-imo had responded to my message. So far, nothing. Then again, she hadn't posted anything since last Tuesday, so maybe she just wasn't logging on this week. I tried not to read into it too much.

In the meantime, my friends took over my classes for the week, teaching two hours every day instead of just one. Occasionally, when they didn't know the answer to a social studies question, they texted me, and I tried to answer right away. I felt bad for creating more work for everyone else. So I studied even harder, looking things up on the Internet or asking Carolina if I couldn't figure out something myself.

When Friday finally came, I braced myself as I walked into

my first-period science class. I felt a lot more prepared for the test than I did for the quiz, but I still felt nervous. So much depended on this one exam! My ability to continue tutoring with my friends . . . my ability to go to Starscape . . . I gritted my teeth as I sat down in my seat.

Right before I put it on silent, my phone buzzed.

GOOD LUCK WITH THE SCIENCE TEST, GIGI!!! It was Zeina, texting in the Ace Squad group chat.

YOU CAN DO IT!!! texted Carolina.

GOOOOOOO, ACE SQUAD! Emma came in, adding a raised hands emoji.

My friends all flooded the chat with different hands emojis, making me laugh. Somehow they'd all remembered the goofy cheer I'd made them do on the first day of tutoring.

Filled with love for my friends, I turned off my phone and got ready as Mr. Roberts started passing out the exams. The one good thing about the test was that, unlike the quiz, it was multiple choice, which meant the grades would be up sometime after school, before Mr. Roberts went home for the weekend.

Hoping I could get a high enough grade to convince my parents to let me keep the squad, I took a deep breath and started the test.

Seventeen

The test, in my opinion, went as well as it could. I didn't freeze up. I answered all the questions before time was up. And I was confident that I'd at least passed when I turned in my exam packet. Now all I could do is hope for the best.

That afternoon, Mom picked up Tommy and me from our schools and drove us to Emma's house. Along with my mom and my dad—who was going to drop by later after briefly closing up the shop—my friends' parents were coming to help set things up.

"It's the best way to get all the parents to show up," Carolina had said while we made the final touches to our plans. "If we tell them that we need their help, they're more likely to come than if we say we don't need them."

She was right, because somehow, despite how busy they usually were, all of our parents said they could make it to the party.

Since we had a lot of younger kids like Tommy and his friends coming, we decided to do a macaroni art night. We figured it was perfect since it was a fun activity everyone could do whether or not they were good at arts and crafts.

I already knew Zeina's and Carolina's parents since I was over at their houses all the time, but today was my first time meeting Emma's.

"Welcome, welcome!" said Ms. Chang, Emma's mom, as she opened the door for us. Ms. Chang was wearing a fancy black-and-white dress, like she was hosting a formal dinner. When she spoke, she drew out her syllables so much that the words sounded extra fancy. "We're so happy you're here! Emma has so few friends. . . . My husband and I were so glad to hear she's finally found a group of nice girls to hang out with!"

Remembering what Emma said about how her parents wanted her to socialize more, I gave her my best smile. "We're so glad to be friends with Emma!" I said. "She's a great addition to our club. Thanks for having us, Ms. Chang."

"Yeah, thanks a lot!" exclaimed Tommy.

"It's my pleasure!" she replied.

When we came into Emma's kitchen, I gasped. On the dining room table and kitchen counters were countless boxes of different colored macaroni.

"Wow, that's a lot of macaroni!" Tommy yelled. He rushed over to look at the various colors.

Emma was standing by the table, her hands full of even more boxes. "I think my mom got a little too excited . . . ," she said sheepishly.

"I didn't want anyone to say we didn't have their favorite color!" Ms. Chang exclaimed. "You don't want people to think we're bad hosts, do you?"

"These are great!" Mom exclaimed. "We brought glue and paper."

When Zeina, Carolina, and their parents showed up, we set up stations all around the kitchen, dining room, and living room. We weren't quite sure how many people would come to the party, but we wanted to set up enough supplies just in case.

At 5 p.m., people started trickling in. Mom and my friends' parents moved to the kitchen table at the back of the room so they could talk among themselves.

Some of the older kids—like Paul and Benny—came with their friends, while the younger ones—like Carly and Kevin—came with their parents. It was weird seeing the parents of the kids we taught!

But what was even weirder was seeing Paul and other people from our grade at *our* party. Just like I'd hoped he would, Paul had brought a bunch of his friends. These kids were all popular, so much so that I wasn't even sure that, besides Caleb and Paul himself, they knew we were alive. But today they actually waved at me and my friends. Did this mean we were cool now?

Once we had a good number of people show up, we started making our macaroni art designs. My friends and I sat on the barstools at the kitchen counter with our pieces of paper. I was so glad that Ms. Chang had brought so many different colors of macaroni. The possibilities were endless!

Zeina made a cute flower with a yellow middle and pink petals, while Carolina made a blue rocket blasting off into the black night sky. Meanwhile, Emma was using black macaroni to make a haunted house with a black cat, and I used all the colors of the rainbow and more to try to make my characters into macaroni stick figures. All our individual styles were coming out! It was really fun.

Dad arrived, and I took him to where Mom, Tommy, and Tommy's friends were making their macaroni art.

"Wow," Dad said, looking around the room. "This is a lot more people than I thought it'd be! You girls taught this many people?"

He sounded impressed, which made me very proud.

"Well, some of the people here are our students' parents, siblings, or other friends that we haven't taught yet," I admitted. "But they're all related to the Ace Squad in some way!"

Laughter filled the room, and I was happy to see that everyone was enjoying themselves. I was heading back to my friends when I met eyes with Paul. He said something to his friends and then walked toward me.

When he was closer, Paul took out a packet from his backpack and showed it to me. It was the math test we took last week. It had a big red 75 on it!

"I thought about texting you when I found out my grade, but I figured it'd be better if I showed you the test itself," Paul explained. "It's not the best score, I know. But I passed! And I was able to at least try all the questions instead of just feeling like I was floundering the entire time."

Pride swelled inside my chest, for Paul, but also for myself. We'd done it!

"Congrats!" I exclaimed. "That's still a huge improvement! You should be so proud of yourself. Does this mean you can stay on the team?"

"For the time being, yeah! My class average still isn't that great, and I'm sure my parents would be happier if I got an A or a B, but Coach is giving me time to bring my grades up. So I'll definitely need more help to bring up the average until I'm well out of the danger zone."

"That makes sense," I replied.

It'd have been easier to just say nothing about what had happened between Carolina and me, or with me and my parents, to pretend that I could just keep tutoring Paul like I wanted. But it wouldn't be fair to anyone. I was lucky I could understand the previous unit so well, but what if I couldn't understand the next? I was already having such a hard time with science. Math could very well be next.

So I took a deep breath and said, "I have to tell you something. Even though I was able to help you out this time, I probably can't help you out anymore. If I'm being totally honest, I'm not good at math normally. I just happened to be good at this unit. And my friend Carolina . . . well, there's a reason she's the regular math teacher. She's the real math ace. You should go with from now on."

Plus, I don't know if I'll even be there for the next time you need help, I added in my head.

Paul frowned. "Oh, are you sure? You were so great this time around, though. You actually made me want to learn math."

"Carolina is an excellent tutor too, I promise," I replied. I was sad, but I tried my best to remain professional. "I've heard nothing but good things from her students. She's funny and smart, too."

"Well, okay."

I expected Paul to walk away from me and rejoin his friends, but instead, he stayed and continued. "Can we still hang out sometime, then? Not through tutoring, but, like, go to the mall and do other fun things."

I gasped. Was Paul Kim Wiley asking me out? I glanced over to the back of the kitchen, where my parents were currently talking to Zeina's parents. They weren't looking at me, but I had a *feeling* that they were listening in on our conversation. Dad's eyebrows were raised, which was a dead giveaway.

"Sure, but only after you get your math grade up," I replied. "You can get that B average. I believe in you!"

Out of the corner of my eye, I saw Mom smile.

Paul laughed. "Way to give me more motivation than I already have! But okay, sure. The first thing I do when I bring my class average out of the danger zone will be to ask you out on a date."

He winked and walked away.

Although I was so happy that Paul asked—or was *planning* to ask—me out, I felt a pinch of anxiety. What if he forgot about me after spending a lot of time with Carolina? What if, by the time he brought up his grade, he was no longer interested?

In the end, I decided to shove all that fear aside. I had way bigger problems right now.

I was checking my phone to see if Mr. Roberts had posted our test grades yet when a lady tapped me on the shoulder.

I turned around to see Kevin and Felicity flanking either side of her. They both gave me a friendly wave, and I waved back at them.

"Hi," she said. "I'm Diane Smith, the twins' mom. I just wanted to thank you so much for helping Kevin. We actually tried getting him tutoring from other places, but things didn't go so well. I heard that there was . . . a rough start for him and the Ace Squad, but his dad and I are so grateful that you stuck with him and helped him with his assignments. He seems to like tutoring now, which is a first for him."

"It's no problem at all," I replied with a smile. "I'm so glad I was able to help Kevin, and he's welcome to come back any time he needs more help."

"Thank you!"

The Smiths went to say thanks to Zeina for teaching Felicity, and another parent came up to say hi to me. Carly had her arms around his waist and was clinging to him like a monkey as he said, "Hey, I'm Carly's dad, as you've probably guessed. I also just wanted to say thanks for all you did for Carly. I hope you'll continue to help her because she enjoys her sessions with you a lot."

I bit my lip, trying not to let my eyes get all misty as I looked at Carly smiling up at me. I *really* liked teaching her, and I hoped I could do it again too.

"Thanks for telling me!" It took every ounce of effort to keep my voice bright and cheery. "I'm so glad to hear that. Hope you and Carly have a fun rest of your night!"

I quickly turned away so they couldn't see the tears that had snuck out of the corners of my eyes.

A couple of more people said hi, and then I glanced back at Tommy and my parents. The three of them had combined four pieces of paper so they had enough space to make a big green T. rex. Tommy was having so much fun, he was gleefully screaming, and my parents—who rarely laughed these days— were laughing too.

Seeing them like this made me smile. Regardless of what my parents decided at the end of tonight, I was glad they were here and having fun.

And then, finally, I turned back to my friends. Carolina, Zeina, and Emma had all finished their macaroni art, which sat side by side on top of our table as they laughed and talked.

Even though we didn't always get along, I was so proud of my friends and me for everything we did to work toward our dream of going to Starscape.

And in that instant, I knew that after everything we'd been through, I couldn't let them miss out on the chance to go just because something happened to me.

"Hey, guys," I said as I rejoined my friends.

My face must have looked really serious, because everyone snapped their attention to me.

My voice shook a little as I continued. "So, I was thinking . . . if I end up failing my science test . . . or my parents still end up saying no after all this . . ."

"No," Carolina said, shaking her head.

"Huh?" I stepped back, confused.

"If, for some ridiculous reason, you do badly on your test even after the full week you spent studying. Or if your parents say no . . . we're not continuing the squad without you. Even though, yeah, sometimes you got too ahead of yourself—"

"And we had to threaten you with a guillotine," Emma cut in, nodding sagely in a way that made us all giggle.

"—and *Emma* had to threaten you with a guillotine," Carolina added, making us laugh even harder. "At the end of the day, there would be no Ace Squad without you, Gigi. And I'm sure I'm not the only one who feels that way. If this plan fails, we can figure out another way to raise money for Starscape. And we can help you get your science grade up."

Emma and Zeina nodded.

"Yup," Emma said. "I mean, I don't know much about science, but for money . . . we haven't even tried learning underwater basket weaving and selling our baskets on Etsy yet!"

"I . . . don't think that's an actual thing that people do," Zeina said. "Isn't it just a figure of speech?"

Emma shrugged. "Maybe. Or maybe not. My point being, I agree with Carolina. We still have plenty of time to come up with a new idea! And Gigi has time to bring up her grade before the semester ends."

Carolina and Zeina made sounds of agreement.

I opened my mouth to respond, but nothing came out. I was too overwhelmed! So instead, I put my arms out at my sides. With knowing looks, Carolina and Zeina immediately hugged me, and Emma joined in.

Even though I was so happy and grateful that my friends said they were all in this together with me no matter what, I hoped we could keep the squad. We'd worked so hard for it to all go crashing down now!

"Thanks, guys," I said. "Let's hope we can stick with the original plan, though. I suck at weaving."

My friends laughed and squeezed me even tighter.

I was about to go join my family and their T. rex making chaos when my phone buzzed.

I checked the notification. Mr. Roberts had posted the grades to our tests!

Eighteen

A small squeak escaped from my lips.

My friends all gathered around me, which made everyone else near us do the same.

I clicked on the notification and pulled up my online grade book.

Next to the words "Unit 3 Reactions Test" was . . .

"A ninety-one!" I yelled. "I got a ninety-one on the test!"

Everyone cheered, even the people who—I'm sure—had no idea what I was talking about.

My friends whooped and cheered, hugging me again.

Just like that, I was one step closer to going to Starscape. Or, at least, I hoped I was. My parents came up to talk to us.

My friends and I all went silent, tense with anticipation.

"Good job, Gigi," Dad said. "Your umma and I are very proud of you."

"Yes, we're so relieved to hear that you were able to bring your grade up," added Mom. "We're definitely going to take this into consideration when we make our final decision at the end of the party."

At the end of the party? It took all my self-control to not complain. If I said anything out loud, my parents would probably think I was talking back. I was so close to getting my parents to approve of the Ace Squad. I didn't want to mess things up now.

"Okay," I finally said. "Hope you enjoy the rest of the party!"

When my parents went back to sit with Tommy, I heaved a big sigh. Out of habit, I logged onto Min-seo's Instagram and checked the conversation with Yeji-imo.

The words "seen 12 h ago" were now below my message! Aunt Yeji had left me on read!

Maybe she just got too busy to reply . . . , I thought. But part of me was tired of making up excuses. Even though I looked up to her a lot, the reality was that I didn't know what Yeji-imo was really like. And at this rate, I wasn't sure if I could even raise enough money to go to Starscape.

I kind of wanted to cry, but I took a deep breath and tried

to focus on what was going on around me instead.

Tommy laughed at something Dad said. Kevin and Felicity were actually getting along while making their macaroni tower. And Paul and his friends were excitedly yelling about the macaroni football that they were trying to make.

I let out my breath, and it came out as a big sigh.

"You okay?" Zeina asked.

I glanced up to see my friends giving me worried looks. And at that moment I realized that, in the end, it didn't matter whether or not Aunt Yeji wanted to meet up with me in NYC. Sure, I wanted to see her if I could, but what really mattered was my friends and us going to Starscape together so we could get closer to achieving our dreams.

"Yeah," I replied, giving my friends a hug. "Thanks for everything. No matter what happens next, I'm so grateful for all of you."

"We're so grateful for you too!" Emma said. "Duh! Can we move on from this sappy moment and go back to enjoying the party now?"

Everyone laughed.

"Sure," I said. "Let's enjoy today the best we can!"

The rest of the party, at least, went well. Everyone had lots of fun, and by the end of it all, a lot of kids from our school asked my friends and me for more information about the Ace Squad, just like we'd hoped they would.

After all the guests had finally left, my friends and I stayed behind at Emma's house with our parents to help clean up. The macaroni art night was fun, but boy had things gotten messy! It took over an hour to clean everything up, even with the big group of people we had helping out.

When all the macaroni and paper were picked up and put into the trash, Dad said, "Okay, the other parents and I have been conversing, and especially now that Gigi's test grade has been posted, I think it's finally time for us to make a decision about the Ace Squad."

I bit my lip and glanced at my friends, who also looked nervous. All we could do now was hope for the best!

"Gigi's mom and I had our doubts," Dad continued. "But we have to admit it. It's amazing that you girls created this community of kids helping other kids. Maybe this club is worth keeping after all."

"However," Carolina's mom said. "We've talked to the other parents and asked them about what sort of things they want to be different. One of the complaints was that there is no adult supervision during sessions. So I think what we parents need to do is take turns supervising sessions at the library so that things don't get out of hand."

"My parents said they'd help out too?" Emma asked, looking shocked.

"Of course, we'd love to!" Emma's mom exclaimed. "Emma, sweetie, we may have a lot of things going on, but we always want to do our best to make time for you!"

Emma wrinkled her nose. At first I thought she was grossed out, but her eyes became shiny. She was trying not to cry! Because I didn't want to embarrass her, I glanced over at Zeina's dad, who looked like he had things he wanted to say too.

"Of course, all of you girls have to keep up your grades," he said. "You can't expect to continue teaching others if you don't do well in school yourselves. Plus, an extracurricular that gets in the way of schoolwork does more harm than good."

Zeina groaned and whispered so only my friends and I could hear, "He heard that from the school counselor when my sisters were applying for college."

I bit my lip to stop myself from smiling.

"That all sounds good," I replied. "Thank you."

"So . . . ," Emma said after a while. "This is probably an obvious question, but just to make sure, this means we get to keep the Ace Squad, right?"

"Yes," Mom said, giving us all a big smile. "You can."

LYLA LEE

My friends and I jumped up and down in excitement. We'd done it!

Before we left, Emma, Carolina, Zeina, and I gathered up our macaroni art and, with Emma's parents' permission, hung them up on the walls. Our designs were so different that it was cool but also kind of funny to see them together. And that was what our club was like! We were all very different people, and sometimes not everything went together perfectly, and we didn't always see things the same way. But together we still made a good, cool thing that could help other people and ourselves. And that was what was important in the end.

It'd been only one month since we started the Ace Squad, and so much had happened already! We had no idea whether we could reach our goal of raising enough money for art camp or if all of us could even get into Starscape. And I still had no idea if things would work out between me and Paul or if Yeji-imo would ever reply to me. But I'd just have to take things one day at a time. . . .

After all, my friends and I got through our first zany month as the Ace Squad. What's to say we couldn't get through the others?

162

Acknowledgments

Middle school, for me, was a pretty wonderful time, not only because it was the first time I went to one school for an extended amount of time after moving every couple of years in elementary school, but also because it was when I was able to form the friendships that would change my life forever. I consider myself truly lucky to have found my first "found family" of friends during these years, meeting people who would continue to play important roles in my life and get me through some of my hardest times. So, Chelsea Chang, Luke Chou, Shiyun Sun, and Bernice Yau, thank you for still being a part of my life throughout all these years. This book—heck, my entire career—wouldn't have been possible without you.

Of course, I also have to thank the friends who have become important parts of my life later on, particularly Annie Lee, Kaiti Liu, Aneeqah Naeem, Alice Zhu, Anita Chen, Francesca Flores, Amelie Wen Zhao, Rey Noble, Stephanie Lu, Angelica Tran, Hester Lee, Huihua He, Linh Truong, Irene Yen, Margaret Zeng, Kris Wong, Alyssa Quinones, Helena Kang, and Brianna Lei (whose games I will forever reference in my books, haha).

Writers like me have this funny little habit of including bits and pieces of the people we love in our books. So, friends, if you spot a couple of details here and there that look familiar . . . haha, you caught me. Whether you've been a part of my life for nearly two decades or for a couple of years, thank you for being my friend.

Additionally, I would like to thank my parents, who questioned but never forbade me from pursuing the zany ideas I had while growing up, whether it was to tutor kids at the library or to write books instead of pursuing more "normal" hobbies. You didn't always believe that I could pull off the whole author thing (and let's be honest, neither did I), but hey! I made it. And thank you for being so supportive of me now. 사랑해요.

Finally, thank you to my amazing agent, Penny Moore, and my equally awesome editor, Alyson Heller. Can you believe the three of us have been on this journey together for five years (six, when this book comes out) now? I've been blessed to have such wonderful and badass Asian American women in my corner from day 1 of my publishing journey. Thank you from the bottom of my heart, for everything!

About the Author

LYLA LEE is the bestselling author of YA books about K-pop and K-dramas as well as the Mindy Kim series and the Gigi Shin books for younger readers. Her books have been translated into multiple languages around the world. Originally from South Korea, she's lived in various cities throughout the United States, worked various jobs in Hollywood, and studied psychology and cinematic arts at the University of Southern California. She now lives in Dallas, Texas. Visit Lyla at lylaleebooks.com or on social media (Instagram, Twitter, and TikTok @literarylyla).